Deirdre floated toward her on a billowy pink cloud, draped in gossamer sheaths and dappled with dewdrops. Jaffey watched, breathless. At the corner of the dream, she saw herself, hesitant and red-cheeked and rigid in the uniform of a cadet. Deirdre called out. The words echoed in her head. *Come to me. Come to me.* Jaffey stepped forward tentatively, afraid the rough fabric of her tunic would shred the iridescent splendor. She reached to take her in her arms but Deirdre was staring past her, her lips parted in erotic rapture. Morgan Quade alighted at her side, like a large swooping bird from the heavens. She enfolded Deirdre in her arms and disappeared with her into a puffy pink fog. Jaffey lay on the bed and watched as they made love in the splendid shadows. Her heart pounded.

She was left alone in her dream, standing at the edge of a desert crater while the sky turned into a sheet of bleak blue metal. A wolf howled in the distance.

Jaffey pointed toward the dream recorder. "I was so close to making love to her," she said, chagrined. "You would hope to have the edge in your own dreams at least."

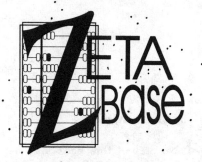

BY
JUDITH·ALGUIRE

The Naiad Press, Inc.
1991

Copyright © 1991 by Judith Alguire

Printed in the United States of America on acid-free paper
First Edition

Edited by Christine Cassidy and Katherine V. Forrest
Cover design by Pat Tong and Bonnie Liss
    (Phoenix Graphics)
Typeset by Sandi Stancil

Library of Congress Cataloging-in-Publication Data

Alguire, Judith.
    Zeta base / by Judith Alguire.
        p.   cm.
    ISBN 0-941483-94-0 : $9.95
    I. Title.
PR9199.3.A368Z4   1991
813'.54--dc20   91-23648
                                                                      CIP

I dedicate this book to my family:

My partner Susan
My sisters Bev and Carrie
My brothers-in-law Bernie and Peter
My nephews Allison and Matthew
My beagles Kate and Emma
My cat Chumbly (Alas there is only one of her)

Acknowledgments

I would like to thank Becky Ellis, Lauren Wright Douglas and Katherine V. Forrest for their helpful criticism and thoughts as the work progressed and Christi Cassidy and Katherine V. Forrest for a fine editing job.

About the Author

Judith Alguire lives and writes in Kingston, Ontario, Canada. She shares an old house downtown with two beagles, two fiddler crabs, a goldfish, one snail and an eighteen-year-old cat. She has a passion for sports of all kinds, particularly baseball and women's hockey. *Zeta Base* is her second novel.

Chapter 1

The guidewires inched steadily from the belly of the gyrocraft, lowering her slowly into the yawning chasm. Beneath the visor her face glowed. Although she had entered the mouth of a volcano many times, she still felt the excitement. The probability of dying in the pit was calculated to be one in ten. For a veteran like herself, the odds were greatly increased. Death had become almost certain, a dark curtain against which she felt curiously alive.

The volcano flared, lashing out in a stream of liquid fire. On the guidewire, Morgan Quade twisted her body so that she was moving about the rim of the volcano in wide pendular arcs. At arm's length, the sea swirled in an angry ancient conflagration. Morgan Quade swam against the red tide.

The volcano began to spit small, hot pellets from the periphery. They looked like a swarm of angry bees. Morgan dropped into a hangman's dance then began to twist like a rag doll.

Suddenly, the body came to life in a saucy backflip.

It was late summer and dusk was falling over the northern hemisphere. The sunset, nestled in a bank of clouds, bathed the western sky in a dull rinse of dreary ochre and dusty rose.

Antiquity loved this time of day, this lull between the day's work and the evening's inevitable social activities. It was her custom to leave her quarters high over the science complex and, after paying a brief visit to Deirdre, make her way to the courtyard. There, she would sit on a bench near the gravel path and commune with her trees until the sun had long set and it was quite dark.

The sun should have shone brightly throughout the day and set later than six o'clock, in a flaming orange ball — for it was the northern hemisphere and it was still summer.

That was the way the sun behaved in ancient times. Antiquity had read descriptions of these events. She relied on computer models and theoretical mock-ups — scientific guesses about what the world must have looked like before the crash —

for most of her visual information. There was some objective evidence, although it was very old — still photographs and a few paintings fashioned from earth pigments, crude but wonderful pictures full of light and brightness. There were even a few centimeters of poor quality film — a few frames saved from the millions that had disintegrated through neglect after the crash. It was a crime, Antiquity thought, that so much had been lost. It was no one's fault of course. No one had had the will or the resources to maintain the archives. All efforts had had to be directed to the urgent task at hand: survival.

If the crash had occurred suddenly, Antiquity thought soberly, no one would have survived. As it was, the world had had years to adapt, years to plan resource allocation, years to devise schemes to enhance the greenhouse effect, hence preserve heat and prevent catastrophic freezing.

Then the sun had dimmed dramatically. That was five hundred and thirty years ago.

Many died of starvation but fewer than had been feared. Many were spared thanks to a system of food distribution blessed, for once, by administrative competence and integrity.

It was a time of suffering and confusion for the animals of the world. Unsettled by the diminishing powers of the sun, they ceased to breed. The effects of the famine were thus mitigated, though scarcely so. Some said it was Earth's greatest hour. For in a time of scarcity, humans collected as many animals as possible into sanctuaries and shared with them the dwindling food supply. Still, shocking numbers of species were driven to extinction.

3

Fortunately, by the time of the crash, humans were no longer dependent upon the soil for food production. Hence, the race was spared the heartbreaking prospect of competing for grass blades with the mice and rabbits — the only creatures who seemed to find the new conditions marginally compatible. For centuries, crops had been grown by hydroponics, fueled by bands of ultraviolet lamps charged by solar disks. After the crash, these efforts were strained to the limit to provide even a fraction of the former crop.

The trees died too, or might as well have. The great forests of the world, deprived of the sun's energy, turned to niggardly swaths of dense underbrush. A few trees did survive in their former grandeur, existing in oases at the half-dozen scientific sanctuaries throughout the globe in association with the animal havens, close to the areas of maximum habitation, sustained by intense concentrations of chlorophyll, manufactured synthetically and fed into trochars situated at the major bifurcations.

The crash had changed the nature of the world irrevocably. There had been problems adjusting the greenhouse effect and, consequently, widespread flooding. Whole island nations had disappeared. Famine and disease were a constant threat in those early days but, finally, they too were overcome, defeated by human intelligence and human cooperation. It was as if the species had faced adversity as one person, had taken a deep breath and decided to be brave.

Antiquity sighed and looked upward into the branches of the great trees. She loved the ancient, giant beasts, loved their majesty and their dignified sympathy for the human condition. When the wind was light, they seemed to whisper, gossiping among themselves about the absurdities of times past. Tonight, they were still and silent. Between their leaves, Antiquity could see the stars, round and cool and twinkling, so many light years away.

The sun was supposed to last for ten billion years.

A chronometer in the square some distance away struck a single pure note — Tchi on the Jupiter scale. It was seven o'clock. Antiquity rose wearily, gathering her robe about her in the slight chill of the summer evening.

The sun had almost disappeared. It hung perilously low on the horizon in a faint violet haze. The remainder of the sky was as black as the deepest night.

Antiquity turned down the garden path toward her quarters. She started slowly, limping slightly until she found an even stride.

Jordan Thyme — Antiquity — was one hundred and fifty-three years old.

Morgan Quade swept into the news center at five minutes past seven and deposited her camera bag on a bench beside the nearest console. She punched in a code number and turned triumphantly to the senior editor who had just emerged from his office.

"It was brilliant, Morgan," he said as she beamed at him. "Rave reviews have already begun to pour in from every corner of the universe."

She had come directly from location and still sported the khaki fatigues she had worn under the silver flight suit. The fatigues were her trademark.

"You have never done anything better," he murmured.

She laughed, a short laugh of glee and relief, running one hand through a mop of short, thick curls. The action seemed to release a pungent smell of other-earthly vapors. She still smelled of the fire and brimstone. It was only when she turned directly toward him that he noticed the dull red mark over her left eyebrow.

"You have a burn," he said, scowling. "You were too close. I don't like it when you get burns."

She looked at him and laughed. "Nonsense, you love it. It's a story in itself: Morgan Quade returns from Io. See Morgan Quade step off the shuttle, the smoke of hell and the scars of battle fresh upon her." She raised her arms dramatically, then paused and looked away, subdued. "Damn it," she said, her voice dropping to a gravelly whisper. "I hate it. I missed them, Alf. I missed the wars."

"What do you know of the wars," he said crossly. "What have you beyond a few old photographs?"

"I can imagine, Alf," she murmured. "To fight the good fight, to die the good death. What could be more glorious?"

"War was primitive," he said primly. "It was uncivilized."

"Well, I'm primitive and uncivilized." She blurted the words, then sank into a chair in front of the console. The display on the monitor was her film. She watched it hungrily.

"It's wonderful," Morgan said.

He looked at her, loving and hating what he saw — the wild smoky black curls, the face burnt a rich umber from too many encounters with the furnace, the gray-green eyes like spitting emeralds. Life for Morgan Quade, he knew, was all about volcanoes and hot, swirling gases. She burned with the intensity of those who were inspired or mad or both.

"Yes, it's wonderful," he said after a moment. He reached over her shoulder and turned off the monitor. "Hurry along now," he said fussily, "or you'll be late for the gala."

Delphi Norbert was the best party-giver on the planet. Some attributed her success to the ambience she created. After all, what guest could fail to be charmed by a view from a cliff that fell three hundred feet to the ocean?

Antiquity was the first to arrive. She brought Deirdre, whom Delphi whisked away at once to show her some flowers she had managed to grow in a rock garden at the rear of the building. Antiquity took an herbal beverage from a tray on the sideboard and stepped through the wide French windows onto the balcony.

The ocean lay beneath her, shimmering in the light of a half-moon. She moved to the edge of the balcony and leaned against the railing. Except for the pale path of the moon and the dim artificial lighting in the courtyard, the evening lay as black as the most remote part of the wild countryside. She preferred the night to the day. It seemed more natural.

"Antiquity, the great science-philosopher! It seems entirely appropriate to find you here, staring at the heavens, contemplating the fate of the universe."

Antiquity turned slowly. Morgan Quade stood in the doorway, a glass lifted to her lips, her gaze fixed on Antiquity with amused interest.

Antiquity said, "Good evening, Morgan," rather coolly. Morgan was her protégé, as were Deirdre and Jaffey, the engineer. Like them Morgan had been selected, even before inception, to be her pupil, to be educated and nurtured. While she had chosen Deirdre and Jaffey partly out of sentiment — Deirdre was her biological granddaughter and Jaffey's biological parents were old friends — she had selected Morgan because her genetic antecedents told her she would be without peer. In her heart she loved Morgan but she resented her relationship with Deirdre. She resented her as she would any interloper.

"Your work on Io was quite excellent," she said. Then, in answer to the unasked question, she added, "Yes, Deirdre is here. She is with Delphi in the garden."

Morgan did not go immediately to the garden, but wandered back into the reception room. Antiquity watched her as she walked slowly along the walls, inspecting the prodigious collection of objective and subjective prints. They were, without exception, the work of Morgan Quade.

Antiquity smiled a trifle bitterly. Morgan, she realized, was arrogant, but with great justification.

8

* * * * *

The President arrived at eight-thirty. She was, at sixty, a young person with an upright bearing and ready smile. The President had the dubious distinction of having been elected by the smallest percentage of the popular vote in the history of the Union. A product of the remote planet Asgard, she was not well-known on Earth; she owed her confirmation to the Union Council to the Middle Colonies whose delegates had lined up solidly behind her and had also lobbied vigorously to deliver the majority of the delegates of the scattered settlements of the Old Colonies. The other candidates — all from Earth with the exception of a fringe candidate from the space station Orca — felt that the Colonies had ganged up on them. But there was no point in complaining. In the Union Council, each settlement large or small had a single vote, a principle of equality which was the very foundation of the Union and jealously guarded by its smaller members.

At the President's arrival the small crowd of guests gathered about Antiquity began to slide away. Antiquity was left alone save for her old colleague, Nadril.

"It's a crime such a person should be in charge of the Union at the half-millennium," Antiquity said bitterly.

Nadril looked at Antiquity bleakly. She was old and crumpled and a little hard of hearing. "I beg your pardon, Antiquity?"

"I said she's not fit to be President," said Antiquity in a loud whisper. "She wasn't born on

Earth or even in the Old Colonies. Never have we had a President whose ties to us have been so tenuous."

"But, she was properly elected, Antiquity," said Nadril timidly.

"She cares not a whit about Earth," Antiquity rasped. "She has nothing but the most superficial intellectual appreciation for us. She speaks of us as if we were some insignificant outpost."

"Many speak of Earth that way," said Nadril sadly. "I think one has to be born on Earth to truly love her — or, at least, be vigorously steeped in her lore and a romantic at heart."

"She balks at everything I propose," said Antiquity testily. "Past Presidents have always looked to Earth as the jewel of the universe. What do we hear from her? Progress, progress, progress. Future-linked budgeting. Rationalization of resources."

"Money is scarce, Antiquity."

Antiquity glared at Nadril. "It wasn't scarce when they elected to build Zeta Base. A ridiculous attempt to capture the grandeur of Earth. It cost dearly."

"They say Zeta Base is beautiful," Nadril said doubtfully.

"It's a plastic abomination. Earth cannot be replicated," Antiquity said. She paused, then said wearily, "Nadril, each day I live I feel more desperate, more in despair of Earth's future. Once I dreamed of restoring her to her original state. Now I tremble for her very existence."

Nadril stared off into space with a wistful smile. "There's a place near the Public Library with a small muddy stream. Sometimes I see a little brown frog there — they were once green, I understand. I close my eyes and imagine a sparkling stream with fish." She sighed. "There will be other presidents, Antiquity, other times. Perhaps even green frogs and fish."

Antiquity hadn't been listening. "She's a creature of the Middle Colonies," she said derisively, staring hard at the President. "She's a technocrat through and through, a person without soul. The Colonies are getting rich. They have their mills, their mines, their agriculture. What do they care about Earth? She's just an expense to them. All I hear in the Council these days is expense, expense, expense. The cost of maintaining the greenhouse effect. The cost of transportation. They say we are unfairly subsidized. We're their mother, Nadril. They've forgotten who we are. They build bubble worlds and brag about creating new Earths." Antiquity paused, slightly out of breath. "They're tiny people. Small minds, small souls. And, they've got the perfect President. Her spirit, her vision are as small as Epsilon."

"It's the times, Antiquity," said Nadril soothingly. "She fits the spirit of the times. She's more popular now, I imagine, than she was when she was first elected."

"She remembers birthdays," said Antiquity with a sour smile. "People are like children. They grow weak with excitement at the sign of a gold-embossed message from the President."

By nine-thirty, everyone had arrived except Jaffey and Millgrew. Delphi, who doted on Jaffey, was reduced to panic and desperately wanted to get away

11

to contact Zeta Base to inquire about her departure time and flight plan. She was, however, thwarted at every turn.

"I see you have a new subjective still," announced the art critic from L'Universe, accosting her as she tried to sneak out the side door. "It's a Morgan Quade of course."

"Yes, it's Morgan's," said Delphi, distracted.

The critic peered into the still, then stepped back. "She paints her own destruction into these creations," he murmured. "It's a death wish."

Delphi opened her mouth to excuse herself but, at that moment, the door to the receiving room burst open and Jaffey swept in, Millgrew in tow.

Jaffey's cheeks were rosy, her wiry blonde hair tousled and twisted. Millgrew, although as immaculate as always, looked vexed. Jaffey crossed the room in a few quick strides, greeted the art critic, then wrapped her arms around the beaming Delphi.

"I was worried about you," she said, much relieved. "Why didn't you call? I almost had an emergency team out after you."

Jaffey regarded Delphi happily. "You worry too much," she said. "Minor problems with the vessel. I thought we'd be able to sneak in in the middle of the celebrations and you'd be none the wiser."

"You're forgiven," she said. She looked over Jaffey's shoulder at Millgrew and whispered, "What's wrong with Millgrew?"

"We had a bit of an accident," said Jaffey brightly. "I got us into the wrong black hole. I took the one to the right rather than to the left of Tybrus 2000."

"But, Jaffey, it's uncharted!"

Jaffey smiled sheepishly. "Getting out of it did require an unusually creative bit of navigation," she admitted.

Millgrew, obviously rattled from her narrow escape from the hungry black hole, looked even paler than she had seemed at first glance.

"Medically, it's a miracle we're alive," said Jaffey agreeably. "You would be fascinated to know the facts, Delphi."

She was about to give Delphi an account of the event when she became aware someone was watching her. Antiquity had turned from the balcony railing and was staring at her through the open French doors.

"You come with me," said Delphi, taking Millgrew by the arm. "I'll show you my garden."

By the time Jaffey reached the balcony, Antiquity had turned once again toward the railing. She lifted her head rather grudgingly as Jaffey appeared at her side.

Jaffey ignored the old woman's reticence. She wrapped the frail body in an enthusiastic embrace. "Antiquity," she cried, "how long has it been? It's been too long. I'm sure of that."

Antiquity released herself stiffly from Jaffey's arms. "It's been almost six months," she said sourly, "and even then your visits have been scarcely more than luncheon stops. I don't recall a time when you've been away so long."

Jaffey glanced about quickly, then leaned toward Antiquity and whispered conspiratorially, "I've been very busy lately. You know about Zeta Base."

"I have heard that of course," said Antiquity

abruptly. "I sent a communique as soon as I heard of your election. Have you not received it?"

"Yes, I've received it." Jaffey placed her hands on the old woman's shoulders and looked into her eyes intently. "But it was so formal, Antiquity. *Jaffey, I wish to congratulate you on the occasion of your election to the Union Council.* That is not the sort of note a doting teacher sends her favorite student, nor is it the sort of note a loving patron sends her protégé. The message crackled with tedious obligation."

Antiquity turned away. "You are too talented to waste your energies on politics."

"You said the same thing when I became a pilot and the same thing when I became an engineer," Jaffey countered cheerfully. "I am the greatest pilot in the galaxy, Antiquity. I am also the greatest engineer. I will, naturally, be the greatest politician."

"You should be involved in classical studies," Antiquity said petulantly, "studies to develop your mind for the role of science-philosopher. That is what your supporters and I agreed on. You were sent to me for that very purpose."

"My supporters were wrong," said Jaffey. "You were wrong. I am totally unsuited to your role, Antiquity. I could no more spend my days contemplating the cadence of the ocean than you could guiding a vessel through the worm holes of Duboltern." She looked at Antiquity sadly for a moment, then said with a quick smile, "but what I have learned at your knee will never be wasted. In the universe only the students of Antiquity know how to use an abacus. Who but Antiquity teaches the lore of the ancients?"

Antiquity nodded but without conviction. "So, my daughter," she said, addressing Jaffey in the fashion permitted to patrons and mentors, "how long will you be with us this journey?"

"I don't know," said Jaffey carelessly. "A few days. Perhaps longer. I'm here for the gala of course. I've been asked to spend a few days reviewing the SOLCOM operation."

Antiquity arched one eyebrow slightly. "Really. Is something wrong?"

"Something quite minor, I'm sure. I imagine I could have dealt with the problem from Zeta Base. But since I'm here anyway, it's worth taking a look."

"Of course." Antiquity cleared her throat, then smiled at Jaffey for the first time. "Since you will be here for a few days, you must have dinner with me at least once. I would be disappointed if we could not have that much."

"I would be disappointed if you hadn't asked," said Jaffey. She glanced up to see Deirdre at the opposite side of the receiving room with Morgan Quade, examining a set of three-dimensional stills. "So this is what she has become," she murmured.

"I beg your pardon?"

"I haven't seen Deirdre in years," said Jaffey, enchanted. "She's grown into a beautiful woman. I never imagined —"

Antiquity looked at Jaffey suspiciously. "Of course she's beautiful," she said, annoyed. "She resembles her biological mother. Helen was a handsome person."

"She was always very sweet," Jaffey continued. "But this — classic beauty. The official photographer doesn't even begin to do her justice."

15

"She dislikes being photographed."

Deirdre, conscious of being watched, turned her head. Her eyes met Jaffey's but just for an instant. She flushed and looked away quickly.

Jaffey took a step in Deirdre's direction. But at that moment Delphi rang a small crystal bell and everyone's attention was directed to a lectern at the front of the room.

The President was about to speak.

The President reviewed the history of the Union, then she concluded proudly that the Union had endured for half a millennium. With charity and good will, it would survive and serve humanity well forever. After vigorous applause, the President then presented half-millennium medals of athletic achievement.

Antiquity turned back to the railing and looked out over the ocean at the moon and at the winking stars of the Big Dipper. For an instant, her mind faltered. She could not remember the name of the constellation.

Jaffey did not notice her discomfiture. She was staring hard at Deirdre and Morgan Quade who seemed, at that moment, lost in a world of their own.

Antiquity left the gala just before midnight, earlier than was her custom on such an occasion. Normally, she would linger in a solitary, although conspicuous, spot and, with feigned reluctance, receive the homage of her subjects. They would pass by one by one — she rarely held court to groups —

eager to show their respect, to seek her wisdom or boast of their latest accomplishments. So many of them had been her students; their triumphs were her triumphs. Few people in the universe had not been touched by her great mind. If they had not been her students, then they were students of her students, or protégés of her protégés. They came to her dutifully, reverently.

But tonight everyone was so excited about the anniversary that a number of people had not had the opportunity to pay their respects to her before she departed. And she had neither the energy nor the will to seek them out.

She was proud of her ability to remember faces and names without the necessity of reviewing the guest list in advance. She was especially proud of her ability to understand and speak, at least in a conversational way, every dialect in the universe. But tonight, she had forgotten a name. Oh, she had remembered it after a few seconds of thought. But, for those few seconds, she had stared into a strange face with bewilderment in her eyes. Apparently, the guest hadn't noticed her hesitation, but Antiquity was forced to retreat to the library for a moment of solitude. She returned from the quiet room only to hear a word she didn't understand. At first she assumed the word was an obscure bit of technical jargon from one of the more esoteric dialects. Then the word was used twice more and, with a shock, she recognized it as a common expression in the principal dialect of Eosine.

She had excused herself early. It was the first time she had missed one of Delphi's light shows and she expected that Delphi would coax her to stay.

Delphi, however, had merely nodded sympathetically, asked her a few questions about the duration of her fatigue, and invited her to make an appointment with her office, reminding her she had not been examined for at least four years.

Delphi's reaction was frightening, almost as frightening as the memory lapses themselves. If tonight had been the first time, she might have dismissed the memory loss as a reaction to the excitement of the evening, nothing more serious than a failure in concentration. But yesterday she had forgotten an appointment and, the day before that, had neglected to take in her students' homework assignments.

It was painfully evident that her memory was failing her. Knowing this, she felt angry and depressed. She had been vigorous and healthy all her life. She was one hundred and fifty-three years old and had not required so much as a lens replacement. It had never occurred to her her brain might fail her before any other organ in her body.

She hoped fervently that the memory lapses were temporary. Sometimes they were. Occasional aberrations of memory and logic in otherwise healthy human beings were often put down to ionic differentials or were explained away, less precisely, as "storms."

Deirdre had accompanied her when she left the party. Deirdre knew she was troubled, although she said nothing. They toured the lambing quarters together and Deirdre insisted she stroke each of the new babies. She believed strongly that animals were soothing and healing, and Antiquity could not fault her scientifically.

Afterwards, she asked Deirdre to sit with her in the courtyard. Deirdre hung her head and said no regretfully. Antiquity realized then she was expecting a lover. She didn't press the issue or embarrass her by asking questions. She guessed the lover was — as was frequently of late — Morgan Quade.

She hoped it wasn't Jaffey. She had seen the hunger in Jaffey's eyes. It disturbed her even now, thinking of it. Deirdre was naïve in the ways of the world, but she had been like that as a child, reclusive and quaint and given to ideas, always happy with animals, content to let others go out and have adventures and bring their stories home to her. Jaffey was, by contrast a doer, sensuous and ebullient, a person of great and varied appetites — and, as Antiquity had heard through gossip, cheerfully lustful and carelessly unfaithful. Jaffey, as fond as Antiquity was of her, would not do as a partner for Deirdre.

Jaffey had changed since leaving Earth. She had fallen prey to the glamorous life. She was less respectful, assuming a degree of familiarity unbecoming between protégé and patron — even if the protégé was Chief Engineer of the Galaxy.

Once she had been the most brilliant scientist in the universe in Jaffey's eyes, Antiquity thought. Tonight Jaffey had treated her like a frail old woman, one who should be let out to pasture, not as a respected colleague. She was an old woman, true, but she had a young person's energy. She wasn't often tired. If only her memory didn't fail her . . .

She glanced toward Deirdre's quarters. The light still burned in the bedroom loft but the curtains were drawn.

* * * * *

Millgrew had a crashing headache from the flight incident. She had remained at the gala only out of courtesy to Jaffey. "The guests are beginning to thin out," she ventured hopefully. "Perhaps —"

"Oh it's a bit early for me," said Jaffey carelessly. She cast a hopeful look about the room. "If you would like to take the vehicle, I'm sure I can get a ride back to the hotel."

"It's quite all right," said Millgrew painfully. "I'd be happy to wait for you."

"No, I can get a ride," Jaffey assured her. She frowned, then brightened. "Oh, there's Allyea," she said with relief. "I had hoped she would be able to come. I didn't think it would take that long to repair the relay station." Jaffey gave Millgrew a sisterly pat on the shoulder. "Go home, rest your head and," she added with a wink, "don't wait up for me."

Millgrew stood, looking forlornly at Jaffey, who had already crossed the room into the company of the laughing, red-headed Allyea. "No," she said to herself. "There would be no point in waiting up." She knew from past experience there would be no point at all.

Deirdre lay against the pillows and watched Morgan. Morgan's tongue drifted across her belly and followed the gentle curve between her breasts, leaving the nipples boldly pink and exposed. She arched her back, offering her breast, inviting Morgan. She was already sore from their long and

20

vigorous lovemaking but she couldn't get enough of Morgan. Morgan brought her to orgasm once again with a soft, thorough stroking. They lay together without speaking.

"I have something for you," said Morgan when Deirdre was ready to talk. She turned and reached into the pocket of her fatigues. "Can you guess what it is?" She held the object out to Deirdre in a clenched fist.

Deirdre looked at the curled fingers almost sadly. "How could I guess," she said. She looked into Morgan's eyes and, at their urging, said, "A piece of the wind."

"No!" Morgan opened her fist. In her palm lay a delicate blue-green ring. It reminded Deirdre of ancient paintings of the ocean sparkling through a gossamer mist. She stared at it with pleasure.

"It's very beautiful," she said. Still, she seemed shyly reluctant to take it.

Morgan continued to hold the gift forward. "It's from Janus," she said. "Some of the lava splashed on my flight suit and solidified. Darius was able to make a ring out of it. He did a beautiful job but then he owes me a favor. Who else would bother to collect the weird materials he's so fond of?"

"No one," said Deirdre simply.

"You could wear the ring on your finger," said Morgan, "or perhaps you would rather wear it on your chain."

The chain was made from a precious vein of Medelian gold and Deirdre wore it always. As Morgan spoke, Deirdre fingered it unconsciously. "The chain, I think," she said finally.

Morgan unfastened the chain and slid the ring to

its center. It dangled delicately against the curve of Deirdre's breast as Morgan secured the clasp. Morgan looked at it, smiling. "I prefer it there too," she said. "It's much more intimate."

"I love it." Deirdre studied the ring for a moment then looked at Morgan in gentle admonishment. "I wish you wouldn't take such risks," she said.

"Risk is relative." Morgan turned over onto her back, folding her arms behind her head with a sigh. "Deirdre," she said, "you should have another someone like yourself, someone who doesn't care to wander, a nice stay-at-home lover who won't break your heart by ending up immortalized in a lava flow."

"If I wanted someone else, I could have someone else," Deirdre said quietly.

"I'll die one of these days," said Morgan. "Living the way I do. My number's going to come up, as some would say. I'll make you very unhappy and you don't deserve to be unhappy. I don't want to but —" She sighed and stared hard at the ceiling. "I was born under a bad star — that's my problem — a supernova. When I was a child and Antiquity wanted to scold me she would always refer to the circumstances of my birth." She cleared her throat, altering her voice to imitate Antiquity's tutorial tone. " 'Morgan you were born under a bad star. That's what makes you so wild and undisciplined. You are fortunate. There are places in our world for people who are wild and undisciplined.' "

Deirdre laughed. "I'll take my chances."

Morgan smiled. She eased closer to Deirdre. "You're a woman of steel," she murmured. "Steel in a velvet glove." Her eyes glistened, heavy with

22

emotion and fatigue. "Defender of the hearth. Lover. Mother." She reached out to touch Deirdre's breast, cupping the fullness in her palm, mesmerized by its softness, stunned by the depth of her own emotions. Deirdre drew Morgan to her, cradling her head in her lap.

"Antiquity's right," Morgan went on. "I am wild and undisciplined." She turned and buried her face in Deirdre's abdomen. "I love to wander but I like to come home too — to this place, to you." Morgan continued to talk, her words growing so faint that Deirdre was forced to lean over her to hear.

Finally — past three — Morgan fell asleep, her head still nestled in Deirdre's lap. Deirdre didn't try to move her. She still tingled from their lovemaking. When Morgan returned from the fiery pits she came eager to explore and to be explored. Tonight she had been ravenous as always. Away, she lived for the fire and drank her soul from it. Then she came home, home to Earth to be healed.

Deirdre touched the dark red mark over Morgan's left eye. Morgan winced but did not wake. Deirdre knew the injury would leave a scar, a hard white scar to match the thin line around her neck. Morgan had earned that scar when she had become entangled in a guidewire on Ursus. It was a miracle she had survived the hanging. As it was, her neck was broken and she was saved from suffocation and brain-death only by the alertness of the shuttle navigator.

The scars could have been removed. Delphi had offered to perform the procedure but Morgan never seemed to find the time. Deirdre understood what no one else did. The scars were symbolic of a lover's commitment, a commitment to the wild, untamed parts of the universe.

At four o'clock Deirdre turned off the light and fell asleep, sitting upright against the pillows.

Antiquity didn't see the light go out. She had fallen asleep in the courtyard, stretched out on the ground, her head cradled between the roots of a giant chestnut.

Chapter 2

Antiquity lay on the examining table in Delphi's surgery. Delphi flitted about her, discussing recipes for ambrosia, as she applied various chemical and electronic sensors to test the composition of her body fluids and the condition of each solid fiber. She asked for a history as she worked, although there was no need to; the sensors gave her a reading instantly of every variation that had occurred in Antiquity's body. Delphi, however, liked to talk, and she placed great store in the subjective recitations of her patients.

When the examination was over, Delphi asked Antiquity to wait in her office while she checked and synthesized her file.

"She's forgotten to water something in her herb garden," Antiquity murmured. "The plant will, of course, wither and die if she neglects it one more minute. I, on the other hand, could turn to dust waiting for her." Antiquity nevertheless seated herself on the bench across from Delphi's desk and indulgently awaited the doctor's return.

Delphi entered the office minutes later. She had not yet removed her smock and, to confirm Antiquity's suspicions, there were traces of fresh dirt about the cuffs. She flopped down on the bench beside Antiquity, slightly out of breath.

"How is your herb garden?" asked Antiquity.

"It's wonderful. If I weren't a working person, I would enter my crop in the achievement fair. As it is, I have to use my best specimens on unworthy types like you, Jordan Thyme."

"I am very sorry," she said gravely. "I had not intended to stand in the way of you and first-prize chevron. It would look quite dashing on the sleeve of your smock."

"I am sure you couldn't care less about my chevron," said Delphi. She took a long breath then settled back, looking at Antiquity.

"How were the examinations?" asked Antiquity finally. "What are the results?"

Delphi said, "It's unusual to see a person of your age who hasn't had any musculoskeletal replacements. Most people have had several joint transplants by the time they reach one hundred and twenty years. You are an amazing specimen."

"My biological parents were blessed with longevity," Antiquity said proudly. "And, of course, I have never left Earth. I haven't exposed myself to the stinking vapors and noxious biological products of Oscar or Lazarus or some of the other peculiar substations."

Delphi had pioneered medicine on both Oscar and Lazarus and had the wrinkles to prove it. She had also experienced four lung replacements since inhaling the odious vapors of Kubusk. "Some of us were great fools," she admitted, "traveling without shields, working without filtration devices. If our patients did the same things, we would be horrified. But," she said with a helpless shrug, "we're doctors; we're immune."

She looked away from Antiquity as she talked, a behavior quite out of character. Antiquity looked at her suspiciously. "What did the rest of your examination reveal, Delphi? Why the memory lapses? Are they the result of a failure to concentrate? A preoccupation?"

Delphi looked at the floor, then at Antiquity. "Jordan, the sensors show evidence of deterioration."

"Deterioration?"

"Yes." She sighed, then said bluntly. "You are losing memory cells at an alarming rate. The cells that control reasoning and perception are holding their own but there is evidence that they too have reached a critical point."

"How long?"

"A few months, perhaps. Within the year, all cells will be in a negative phase."

"And then?"

"Within two years, all higher cerebral functions

27

will have ceased. Your capacity to function intellectually, in any meaningful way, will have been compromised long before that. You have, perhaps, three good months."

"I will die," Antiquity said shortly.

"You have two years."

"For all practical purposes, I have three months."

"There are alternatives," she began.

"A brain transplant!" Antiquity turned away angrily. "Look at Lineus! He's three hundred years old. He could live forever, barring an accident that reduces him to powder. He's nothing more than a complicated robot. A child could build him with a birthday kit. We don't know what to do with him."

"We don't know what Lineus feels," she conceded unhappily. "No one alive knew him before the operation. We don't know who he was or how he perceived the world and neither does he. Perhaps we failed. But perhaps we succeeded. Who knows?"

"Nonsense." Antiquity stared at the wall stonily. "Nonsense, Delphi. We have seen the results of similar operations. What is it they all say? They say they feel hollow. And they have all died under the most suspicious circumstances. The soul is an elusive thing, Delphi," she said caustically. "It has proven most difficult to transplant."

Taking Antiquity's hand in hers, Delphi looked directly into her eyes. "Jordan, it is my duty as a doctor to put the option before you. I do not recommend that you accept it."

"Then I will die."

"Yes."

"And I have very little time."

"Very little, Jordan," she said. In the emotion of

that bittersweet moment, she reached out to touch her cheek.

Antiquity held herself away, suddenly rigid with anger.

"Life is not always just, Jordan."

Delphi took Antiquity's hand and led her out of the office, through the dispensary and into the herb garden. This time, Antiquity did not resist her attentions. Delphi walked with her along a wide dirt path, stopping suddenly beside a rose bush, a rare shrub that bore a single bloom of delicate, silvery orange.

"Jordan," she said at last, "I always knew what kind of old woman you would be. I knew you would never go to your end placidly. You were a stubborn, impatient young person — so vigorous. Handsome too, I might add. You couldn't wait for Andronicles to step aside. You chafed at the restrictions she placed upon you as her assistant, restrictions that were largely imagined, if I may be so bold as to say. I remember you muttering about old women who didn't have the sense to step aside for stronger bodies, younger minds. You were ambitious, Jordan, so totally engrossed in your work. You didn't have time for anyone, not even me." Delphi looked away for a moment. "Well, you're a stubborn old woman now," she said shortly, "and still ambitious, still jealous of your status, chafing at the limitations of your own body and mind, still unwilling to see the justice in stepping aside for a younger person. It's a disgrace, Jordan, that you haven't prepared anyone for your role."

Had anyone else said what Delphi had just said, Antiquity would have turned away in fury. But this was Delphi, the woman who had been her colleague for so many years at the great university at Edinburgh, the woman who had been in her life longer than anyone, the woman who had broken her heart by eloping with the mad musician Veta. That, however, was a long time ago and she had long since forgiven her.

"I prepared three," said Antiquity stonily. "Only Deirdre has not refused out of hand although I know the very idea of being in the public eye repels her."

"Perhaps the others knew you would never step aside," Delphi said gently. "They know as long as you live they would be in your shadow. They could not put their lives on hold waiting for you to retire."

"Jaffey has been seduced by technology," Antiquity said sourly. "I knew it was a mistake to let her major in engineering. Morgan won't consider the position because she knows Jaffey was my first choice." She sighed, shaking her head. "There was always a great rivalry between them. I daresay they shaped each other's personalities, created mirror images out of their intransigence."

Delphi nodded, smiling at her memories. "Oh, yes, they were quite the pair of scalawags. I'll never forget one holiday they spent with me. Jaffey spent hours designing an elaborate system of pulleys and counterbalances to scale the cliff off my balcony. Morgan took one look at the plans and said: 'Why don't you just tie a rope to the railing and jump?' Which of course she proceeded to demonstrate."

"Of course," said Antiquity dourly.

"Broke both legs," said Delphi cheerfully. "I can still see Jaffey standing over Morgan's cot in the infirmary, saying in the most scathing tones: 'Why would you do such a thing? You didn't examine the rope to determine its tensile properties. You didn't even know if it was long enough.' "

" 'But I wanted to know how it felt to jump off a cliff on a rope,' Morgan replied. 'How would I know what it felt like if I was certain of the outcome?' That sort of reasoning used to drive Jaffey mad."

"Indeed, it drives me mad to this day."

"And remember how angry Jaffey was when Morgan was accepted at the Academy, stood first in her class, then left after one term to study art with Nurema? Morgan applied only to show Jaffey she could compete on equal terms in her arena. Oh —" Delphi stopped, clapping her hands in delight. "They were wonderful children, Antiquity. I don't think I've ever had as much fun as I did while they were growing up."

"You had them only for the occasional holiday," Antiquity said. "Their rivalry could be rather a trial at times. They competed in everything. They even vied for Deirdre's attention and she loved them both — Jaffey always so bright and amusing. Morgan — well, Deirdre loves her the way she does her undisciplined animals."

"Deirdre lets Morgan show her tender side," said Delphi. "Morgan would never allow anyone else to see that part of her."

"Yes, she turns a hard armor to the world," Antiquity said curtly. "Life has always been difficult for her — she's made it that way — and so easy for Jaffey. Morgan is so sullen. Jaffey is so cheerful. She attracts people to her as readily as Morgan affronts them." Antiquity sighed. "Morgan is an uncut sapphire," she murmured as if to herself, "rough and

31

crude. Jaffey is polished gold — sunlight, moonbeams on the water. Morgan is blackness and night. Even as a baby she liked to explore the dark corners. Jaffey was the child who liked the shiny new things. And Deirdre —" Antiquity looked away to hide her emotion. "Deirdre is the best of the lot, the only one to remain faithful to me."

"They're young, Antiquity," said Delphi softly. "They may seem neglectful but it's just that they have their own lives. They all love you."

"Love me! Nonsense!" Antiquity made a bitter face. "Respect. Duty perhaps. Not love."

"No," said Delphi steadily, "they love you. They know you care for them even though you aren't very good at showing you do. They know under that stern science-philosopher exterior is a wonderful, whimsical child whose greatest dream is to chase a bright butterfly over some grassy sun-drenched hill." She paused, rubbing Antiquity's hands between hers. "That is the side of you I have always loved."

For a moment Antiquity was silent. "Sometimes, I feel a trembling," she said, "a great fear for the Earth."

"Yes," Delphi said patiently, "you've told me about this."

"I have done everything. But what if my efforts are insufficient? What if it's torn from me in the final instant?"

"Jaffey's here to help," said Delphi. "What could go wrong with something entrusted to Jaffey?"

"Yes, yes, I know."

"Then all is well," said Delphi. She took Antiquity's index finger and drew it along one petal of the rose. The touch brought forth a delicate fragrance and made Antiquity want to sob with a strange sense of timelessness and loss.

"Yes," she said finally. "Still —" Her voice trailed off. She swallowed hard and continued. "You must promise," she said, keeping her words clipped to ensure she spoke firmly, "you must promise if I display behavior that is undignified or out of character you will find a way —"

"Of course I will. I hope you would do the same for me."

"If I do not manage the problem, myself," Antiquity added. She inhaled deeply then said, "You understand, Delphi, what we have said here is confidential."

"Of course. It's a matter of physician-patient privilege."

"Good." Antiquity nodded. "I have much to do, and I don't want to appear to be at a disadvantage."

"I am here," Delphi said simply.

Antiquity left through the garden, with Delphi looking after her wistfully. After she had travelled several yards along the walk, she paused to look back. Delphi was bent over the frosty orange rose, her white smock reflecting tones of ailing ochre and flat vermilion in the early afternoon sun.

Antiquity thought: *I'm dying. And if I don't hurry, they will all be dead.*

Chapter 3

"I like them because they're so much like people. I suppose you've heard that many times before."

"And I prefer them because they are not," said Deirdre. She regarded the speaker coolly for a moment then turned back to the great apes and said, "Excuse me, Penny, excuse me, Gottfried. It appears we have an intruder."

Jaffey leaned against the doorframe, smiling. "Since when is an old friend an intruder?"

"Since she interrupts a meal with my favorite companions."

Jaffey refused to be put off. She stepped through the doorway, arms extended. "Deirdre," she said accusingly, "you rushed away from the gala so fast I never had a chance to say so much as hello. It's Jaffey. Remember? Tell me you're glad to see me."

Deirdre returned Jaffey's embrace perfunctorily. "Faces do fade from memory over time," she said lightly. "It's been years since we've seen one another. I'd assumed you'd forgotten I exist."

"How can you say such a thing," Jaffey cried. "How could you imagine I'd forgotten you exist? Why, I've sent you a communication every birthday since I've been away, even when I was marooned on the Sibean Fields."

"Yes," Deirdre acknowledged. "It's always nice to remembered on special days."

Jaffey glanced toward the apes and said in a low voice, "You've eaten with them. Does this mean you won't be joining Antiquity and me this evening?"

"Yes, Jaffey, it means that."

"And I was so hoping you would dine with us." Jaffey dropped her arms to her sides in a gesture of defeat. "Is it too much to ask? To dine with the most beautiful woman in the universe?"

Deirdre looked at Jaffey, disconcerted by the intensity of her scrutiny. "Yes, Jaffey, apparently it is."

Deirdre had turned away so that the afternoon sun caught her to full advantage. Jaffey smiled. She was a study in pastels — her hair, her eyes, even the splash of color in her cheeks. She reminded Jaffey of the watercolors that hung in Antiquity's study — subtle yet vibrant. "You know, you're very beautiful," she said.

"I've never placed much value in physical appearance," said Deirdre sharply. She realized even as the words left her mouth that she had been unnecessarily harsh. "I'm sorry," she said quickly. "I've forgotten my manners. I was about to get Penny and Gottfried some tea. Would you care for something?"

"A glass of iced tea would be nice," said Jaffey meekly. She followed Deirdre into the kitchen.

Deirdre took out a large canister of tea. While she prepared the beverage, Jaffey poked about the shelves, marveling at the wide assortment of animal formulae.

"You have a formula for orphaned bats," she exclaimed. "Does anyone actually feed orphaned bats? Bats are ugly."

"Ugly things feel hunger too," Deirdre said reproachfully.

"Yes." Jaffey stared at the bat formula for a long moment. "What do you mean, Deirdre, when you say you like the apes because they aren't like people? Don't you like people anymore?"

"I like some people," she said coolly. "Others I don't care for as much." She handed Jaffey a glass of iced tea and moved away. "Penny and Gottfried prefer theirs hot," she said to no one in particular.

"It must be strange," said Jaffey. "Mucking about in caves, looking for bats, combing the rocks for reptiles. Does it really matter if we have a perfect census of white snakes? Does it matter if all the snakes are gray?"

"It matters to them," she said stolidly.

Jaffey smiled. "At least one thing hasn't changed. You still get angry when your animals are

36

challenged." She took a long drink from the glass. "Excellent tea. Is it your concoction?"

"No, it's Antiquity's. She's developed an interest in drying and preparing her own teas lately. She's quite skilled although she tries to be offhand about it."

"My compliments to Antiquity," said Jaffey. "How is she?"

"She's well."

"She seemed preoccupied at the gala," Jaffey mused. "Less robust too. I thought I saw age in her face for the first time."

Deirdre looked at Jaffey, distressed. "She's happy," she said quickly. "She's very busy with her work and happy with her trees."

Jaffey shook her head. "I don't understand why Antiquity cares so much about trees. They're nothing more than large plants. I've never seen her wax poetic over a stalk of celery."

"They remind her of how grand Earth once was. They're living monuments to the beauty the planet once held. Earth's still beautiful to Antiquity," she added quickly, "and to me and to many others."

"But it's so dark," Jaffey interrupted impatiently. "To me, beauty is the explosion of colors when a ship jumps to hyperspace or the gleaming white walls of the wormholes. Or the sun over Zeta Base."

"I like Earth," Deirdre said, intractable. "And I like trees. It must be wonderful to be a tree, so wise, so strong. Antiquity's trees are older than she is. She remembers them being in the courtyard when she was a child. They were very old then and as tall as they are now. She cherishes them as friends."

"But they can't feel anything," Jaffey said with a

shrug. "That issue was laid to rest centuries ago. Their emotions turned out to be nothing more than shifts in the protoplasm in response to stimuli."

"Still it's fun to imagine they see and feel," Deirdre persisted. "It's magic. Don't you believe in magic, Jaffey?"

Jaffey shrugged. "What is magic but the failure of science? Look at the ancients. They believed black holes were gateways to heaven. We've navigated countless black holes. We have yet to find heaven."

"Perhaps you haven't found the right black hole," said Deirdre stubbornly. "Perhaps the route to heaven is through a special black hole, one that can be entered only after death."

The sadness in Deirdre's eyes softened Jaffey. "You want to believe that because you have lost so many animal friends," Jaffey said softly. She felt sad but at the same time curiously light-hearted. "Yes, Deirdre," she whispered, "I do believe in magic. What better way to explain the mysteries of the universe."

"What better way indeed."

They turned to see Antiquity standing in the doorway. "You're almost on time, Jaffey," she said abruptly. "According to my chronometer you are only half an hour late. For you, I assume that is being on time."

"I'm terribly sorry, Antiquity." Jaffey stepped forward, holding out an apologetic hand. "I stopped to see Deirdre on my way to your quarters and, as you see, we've fallen into an intense philosophical discussion."

"Of course." Antiquity released Jaffey's hand and

looked toward Deirdre. "You're welcome to join us for dinner, Deirdre."

"It's all right, Antiquity," she said gently. "I've already eaten." She gave Jaffey a quick smile. "Excuse me, Jaffey, I'm neglecting my guests." Deirdre returned to the great apes. Jaffey followed Antiquity across the courtyard to her quarters, a splendid loft on the third floor overlooking the ocean.

Antiquity's quarters were a paradox. The loft itself was a clean, white area of pure space, discreetly housing the latest scientific gadgetry. The gleaming instrument panels and sleek consoles reflected the scientific side of the woman, a side that many — particularly the young — were apt to forget. The sideboards, however, were a clutter, the pristine classic lines obscured by a hodgepodge of curios that reflected the mysterious side of Antiquity, the side regarded as quaint, the side much talked of throughout the universe.

The central table held an ancient wooden telescope and a small, slightly more modern-looking box containing a complicated arrangement of prisms. Jaffey was studying the box when Antiquity said, "Would you like a drink?" Jaffey put the box aside and followed Antiquity to the corner of the room set aside for food preparation.

"I'm glad real food is becoming fashionable," said Antiquity, surveying the steaming pots. "Tablets and concentrates are all very well for travelers and for emergencies and the occasional convenience. But they are quite uncivilized and destroy an excellent opportunity for social intercourse."

"Of course real food does require a separate room

and all sorts of paraphernalia," said Jaffey doubtfully.

"But it's worthwhile." Antiquity held up a plate for Jaffey's examination. It was made of a dense white material, touched with an occasional strain of carmine. "Our renewed interest in food preparation has revived some forgotten arts. This set of dishes for example was made from the seashells that wash up on the beach in front of the compound. The shell has been strengthened naturally by the salt water. The glaze is the distilled vapor of Uranus."

"Very beautiful," said Jaffey.

"The beverage glasses are also made from shell," Antiquity went on. "In this case the shells were pressed by artisans into exquisitely thin sheets then layered and dipped with the same lacquer." She poured a drink into a piece of the stemware and handed it to Jaffey. "Don't worry," she said with a slight smile as Jaffey hesitated, "the material is very strong. It should prove quite durable even in the hands of a vigorous individual like yourself."

She motioned toward the bench at the entrance to the balcony. "Come, sit down. Dinner will be in a little while. It's available instantly, of course, but I prefer to let it brew for a time. I savor the experience. Cooking is something I never took the time for in my youth."

"Is that a message, Antiquity?"

"No, a simple statement of fact." Antiquity pressed a button on a control panel concealed within the window sill. Within seconds, the room was filled with sounds of unusual clarity and vibrancy, seeming to come from every corner of the room, synthesizing at a point three feet ahead of Jaffey and slightly to her left.

Antiquity pushed a second button. The window covering slid aside noiselessly. The ocean beyond reflected the setting sun in a dull flat bronze, accentuated by an intensely red line at the horizon. Antiquity stared toward the red line for a long time. Jaffey sipped her beverage and watched Antiquity without speaking.

"Do you like the music?" asked Antiquity after a time.

"Yes, I like it very much. Venezia, isn't it? Movements of the sun?"

"Which movement?"

"I don't know," said Jaffey carelessly. "The fifteenth, perhaps."

"No, it isn't the fifteenth. Think again."

"The seventeenth, perhaps," said Jaffey patiently.

"No." Antiquity's lips curled into a slightly indulgent smile. Then her face hardened. She turned to the console and impatiently stabbed in a sequence of numbers. "That was Trapnell's seventeenth," she said brusquely. "This," she said, striking the final number, "this is Venezia."

The rhythmic staccato of the corona ceased abruptly. The room was filled instead with a sound so haunting Jaffey was at once reminded of the recordings she had heard of the mighty ocean mammals.

"It's beautiful, Antiquity," she said humbly.

"Yes. It has the fullness and anxiety of the oboe,

the ancient wind instrument I like so much. This arrangement is, however, very recent. It is, in fact, Venezia's latest synthesis."

"Venezia is very talented," said Jaffey. "I apologize, Antiquity. I'm not very good with music. I like everything and recognize nothing."

Antiquity nodded absently. "Trapnell's composition captures the sun in its full vigor. The music is of course very old — Trapnell wrote it over seven hundred years ago. Venezia has tapped the vibrations of a very different sun." She turned away from Jaffey, squinting once again into the thin red line. For a time, she stood very still. Then, as if stricken by some sudden, severe ague, she began to tremble violently. "Jaffey," she said in a choking whisper, "the sun is dying."

Jaffey was staring at a point on the floor just ahead of her left foot, bobbing her head in time to the ballet of the sun spots, her lips parted in concentration.

Antiquity thought she had not heard. "Jaffey," she rasped, "did you hear what I said? The sun is dying!"

Jaffey released herself reluctantly from Venezia's spell. "The sun has been dying for years, Antiquity," she said matter-of-factly. "The Neo-Gregorian calendar is based upon the Great Maunder Minimum. You taught me that yourself. I was two and a half years old at the time. It was, I imagine, my first formal lesson."

Antiquity took a few shuffling steps toward Jaffey, befuddled by her insensibility. "Jaffey," she said as clearly as possible, "the sun is nearer death than we thought. SOLCOM continues to project a steady state but that simply isn't true. The figures don't make sense. There is a serious error in the system."

"Oh." Jaffey stared at the floor with the air of a person coming out of a haze. "Perhaps that's why the President asked me to do the systems check. If there's an error the repercussions would —"

"It was *I* who asked you to do the systems review," cried Antiquity. "About two months ago I noticed a discrepancy between my figures and the data I was receiving from SOLCOM. At first I thought I had made an error. I worked and reworked the mathematics. There is no doubt in my mind. SOLCOM has malfunctioned. I have reported my findings to SOLCOM command repeatedly. The imbeciles treat me as if I were senile. Finally — just yesterday — the President intervened and ordered a systems review."

"How do you know they are in error?" asked Jaffey. She leaned forward intently. "What is your source of independent verification?"

Antiquity went to her desk and took a heavy metal case from the top drawer. She unlocked the case and placed it on the table in front of Jaffey. "This is my verification."

Jaffey placed both hands on the case so lightly that only her fingertips touched the surface. The metal felt very old. She smiled, partly from the sensual pleasure derived from handling the beautifully worn object, and partly out of appreciation for its great age. She said, bemused, "A neutrino counter. One of the very early portable models. I doubt if you could find a scientist today who would place any faith in the veracity of the device, even the most up-to-date models."

"The neutrino count has taken a dramatic downward turn over the past two months," said Antiquity as if she hadn't heard. "This decline is particularly significant since we are now well into the summer solstice." She paused, then added, "There are other signs as well. The hair on Deirdre's animals is thickening at an unusual rate. They are preparing for winter, Jaffey."

Jaffey shrugged. "I am no expert at interpreting animal behavior, but it seems plausible that Deirdre's pets might be responding to some anticipated aberration of minor significance."

"It will not be temporary and it will not be insignificant," Antiquity insisted. "The signs all point to a change that will be abrupt and dramatic. The present neutrino readings are harbingers of disaster."

"But surely SOLCOM —"

Antiquity glared at Jaffey, beside herself with exasperation. "I have told you, the communicator is malfunctioning. I do not trust its intelligence. That's why I sent for you. I want an independent assessment. I want the opinion of someone I can trust. I want you to take the communicator apart, piece by piece if necessary. When the error is discovered, we must be prepared to act immediately. There is very little —" She paused, wheezing.

Jaffey jumped up and bounded to Antiquity's side. She placed a soothing arm around the old woman's shoulders. "That is exactly what I am here to do. And knowing I am here at the request of an old friend will make the task all the more meaningful."

Antiquity turned away, spent. "You understand the implications," she said anguished. "If the sun is, indeed, near death —"

"You would have to leave," Jaffey interrupted brightly. "The task of maintaining the greenhouse effect would be at first prohibitively expensive and then technically impossible. The earth would cool and, ultimately, even the air would freeze. Long before that, of course, glaciation would disrupt most settlements and make life, as we know it, quite untenable."

"I will not leave!"

Jaffey nodded. For a moment her expression was somber. Then she was once again alive with enthusiasm. "You could move to Zeta Base," she said happily. "You've never been to my home planet."

"I have no desire to go to Zeta Base," said Antiquity shakily. "I was against that plastic abomination from the beginning."

"You would love it," said Jaffey, undeterred. "It's like Earth, but smaller. It's —"

"It is but a pale copy," Antiquity cried. "I'll hear no more of it!"

"We even have gravity sports," said Jaffey. "We've built a special stadium."

"Stop the prattle." Antiquity's eyes were frenzied. "I'm trying to tell you we are in grave danger and you're behaving as if we're discussing some esoteric theoretical model. If your review of SOLCOM uncovers the error — and I know it will — we'll have to be ready to act at once."

45

"We have a formal contingency plan," said Jaffey carelessly, "as you well know. It wouldn't take more than three weeks to evacuate Earth. In a pinch — if all went well and we pushed our pilots and equipment to exhaustion — we could complete the exercise in five days."

"I am well versed in all aspects of the contingency plan." Antiquity stumbled to the balcony and stood there, struggling to catch her breath and fight back an overpowering anxiety. *You must be calm*, she told herself, *or she will dismiss you as a hopeless crank*. Finally she turned back to Jaffey and, in a tone as controlled as she could muster, said, "I haven't given the slightest thought to evacuation. I'm working out an alternate course of action. My calculations are almost complete."

Jaffey looked at her mentor, mystified. "Yes?"

"Yes." Antiquity took a few steps away from the balcony and stopped directly in front of Jaffey. Folding her hands behind her back, she said firmly, "We will explode the sun."

For a moment, Jaffey thought Antiquity was joking. She sat rooted to her chair and stared into the old woman's eyes, her mouth caught halfway between a laugh and a smile. By the time she had grasped the fact that Antiquity was perfectly serious, the old woman had turned away.

"My plan is entirely feasible and ridiculously inexpensive," Antiquity went on. She glanced sharply at Jaffey over her shoulder, but Jaffey merely nodded, round-eyed. Antiquity continued, "The sun is composed of numerous layers of dense hydrogen which has an extremely high kindling point." She paused, but Jaffey continued to regard her with bewilderment. Antiquity took a deep breath, coaxing herself into the familiar and comfortable tutorial tone. "As you know, in the third decade immediately preceding the half-millennium, the major powers drained the sun's energy for the purpose of maintaining a certain collection of energy-intensive military space stations. At the time —"

"But that is unproven!" Jaffey sprang to her feet, alert to the smell of debate. "No intelligent being would attempt something so foolish, so monstrously impossible. Over five hundred years ago, we entered a Maunder Minimum. That was the scientists' explanation. Similar solar events had occurred before, perhaps on numerous occasions since the planet was born. There is an ancient story for children that documents just such an event —"

"*The Silver Skates*," said Antiquity shortly. "The theory of the Maunder Minimum has been perpetuated in order to preserve the Union, to diffuse blame," she continued quickly. "When the great powers saw what they had done, they were truly shocked. Being human, perhaps they had the decency to feel ashamed. They were not, however, prepared to receive the reaction from the rest of the world had it been known the solar famine was the result of a foolish chauvinistic fascination with military playthings. The semblance of power, Jaffey," she said severely, "the mere appearance of supremacy was the name of the game."

Jaffey looked at Antiquity, stunned. "But Antiquity, that explanation is merely a theory, a theory riddled with holes — almost a myth. You told us that yourself. In the early days of the Union it was considered rank heresy. You taught us that. You

47

taught us never to mention the theory except in jest."

Antiquity regarded Jaffey. "I lied," she said simply. She walked to the balcony again and glanced over the railing. "The truth of the solar famine was buried at the beginning of the half-millennium. Documents were destroyed. Persons with firsthand knowledge were sworn to secrecy. Those who weren't trusted to maintain silence were killed."

"Killed!"

"Yes, such things were done at that time. Those murders were, perhaps, the last acts of violence committed by our kind." Antiquity moistened her lips, forming her next words carefully. "I taught you and your classmates the theory was a joke for the sake of the Union. National origins and identities are not entirely a thing of the past. There is a touch of provincialism in each of us. It is unwise, generally, to dredge up old sins. I kept the theory alive — when I could so easily have dismissed it — as a matter of ethics. A teacher must teach truth and, if not, must at least hold open the possibility of its discovery. I was taught the theory by my teacher and she by hers, each, I imagine, in the same spirit that motivated me. My students are the elite, the future generation of leaders in the universe. The technicians accept what the computers tell them without question. I taught you to use the abacus, Jaffey, so you would think. I taught you the theory so you would be curious about the truth. Whether you believed it to be true was unimportant."

"Then I am indebted to your integrity, Antiquity, but I don't see how the theory meets your present needs. Does it matter who committed the sin over five hundred years ago?"

"No." Antiquity paused for a moment. "It doesn't matter *who*, Jaffey, it only matters *how*." She glanced toward Jaffey, then began to pace slowly about the room, half-muttering, her eyes fixed on the ceiling. "If the theory is right," she ruminated, "and I believe it is, it points the way to our salvation. If reaching critical temperature is what is necessary to ignite the fuels beyond the thermal layer, the task could be accomplished with relative ease."

"Using a simple dense nuclear pack projectile." Jaffey shrugged. "A charge of not more than forty megacones would suffice."

"Correct. Perhaps not even that."

"What you're suggesting is a dangerous proposition, Antiquity."

"The risk is acceptable. I would suggest the probability of failure is less than two percent."

"Where did you get that figure?"

"I calculated it on my abacus."

Jaffey smiled and set her glass aside. "Remember Arbus," she said with a laugh. "You taught us about him. He wanted to save Earth by moving it into the orbit of a different sun. He planned to insert fifty megacone charges at each pole and explode them. There are too many variables even to make an educated guess about the outcome of Arbus's experiment beyond an almost certain assurance of disaster."

"I am not Arbus," said Antiquity angrily. "I am a serious scientist reporting a significant variation in the neutrino constant to a group of fools." She paused, somewhat mollified by Jaffey's contrite expression. "When you discover the problem at SOLCOM and can verify my results let me know as soon as possible. I'm preparing a proposal for the Council. I'll want to have all the data."

Finally it dawned on Jaffey that Antiquity was perfectly serious. She wanted to tell her kindly and with humor that the neutrino counter was antiquated, that her theories were riddled with holes, pessimistic and wrong-headed. But the old woman's face looked terribly set and, in profile — for the first time — frail and vulnerable.

Jaffey swallowed a smile and said respectfully, "Of course, Antiquity. I'll get the results to you at once."

"Then it is agreed," said Antiquity, her face slack with relief. She turned away for a moment to compose herself, then said, suddenly breathless, "Jaffey, we have very little time."

Alix Windsor was born on the tiny space station of Leith at the far end of the giant black hole of Taurus 5. She had received a routine education on Leith and had gone into Union service at a very young age. Now, at the age of twenty-five, Alix was a full colonel and commanded the entire territorial fleet off planet Xerxes.

It was unusual for one so young, particularly a candidate possessing such routine formal credentials, to achieve such exalted position and responsibility. Alix, however, had proven her worth first as a patrol commander, leading convoys of commercial vessels through the asteroid fields to the mines at the very edge of space, then as the head of rescue operations, salvaging life and property in some of the most dangerous pioneering expeditions in the uncharted colonies.

Life in the remote territories was lonely, and Alix spent most of her free time reading. Her favorite stories were about the planet Earth — vivid, beautiful descriptions, written mainly by the science-philosopher Antiquity, that arrived from time to time on the cargo vessels from the New Colonies. Alix had never been to Earth, and before yesterday, had never met anyone who had been there. But now she had received orders directly from the President, delivered by the President's personal courier. Alix was to command the Territorial fleet on a special exercise. The fleet was to leave Xerxes immediately and rendezvous with Earth Station 1, August 27th, in anticipation of touchdown on Earth. The orders were sealed, only for Alix or, in the event of Alix's death, only to the second-in-command.

Alix, suppressing her excitement, conveyed to the courier that the orders were accepted and understood. The courier had a fresh soil smell about him and evidence of generous age. He smelled the way she imagined Earth would smell.

In less than three weeks, she, Alix Windsor, remote descendant of a great family of Sub-Oceana, would step down to the birthplace of her ancestors.

Anatole Zog received the same President's message and went directly to his quarters. Once there, he broke into a severe asthmatic attack and was forced to resort to the medical officer of the Middle Colonies. Anatole told himself he was allergic to the strange, silent messenger who had arrived so unexpectedly, bringing traces of Earth soil and other pesky allergens into the well-groomed command module of the Second Fleet.

Anatole had gone to Earth once. As a child, he had attended the Science Academy in Western Transcontinenta. He had proven to be so allergic to the place that he was forced to return home and take the remainder of his education from the console. The same thing had happened when he answered his appointment to the Space Academy. While the other cadets spent glorious summers in training off Zeta Base, he was forced to sit in front of a flight simulator, weaving his way through imaginary black holes and mathematical models. When Anatole was installed as fleet commander of the Middle Colonies, a special allergen-free capsule was constructed, and in the capsule, Anatole was able to give at least an illusion of active command.

As soon as the allergy attack was under control, Anatole summoned his attaché and asked that his capsule be prepared at once. The President had ordered the Second Fleet to leave base immediately, rendezvous with Earth Station 1 and hold, anticipating touchdown on Planet Earth shortly thereafter.

Oliva Stern was a graying commander of the First Fleet, the largest command in the universe, encompassing the Earth-based fleet as well as the vessels of the Old Colonies. As the senior commander, Oliva had the most direct line to the President and, through her, to the Union Council. She was responsible not only for representing the philosophies and needs of the First Fleet but also the more remotely based Second and Territorial Fleets. She had a large fleet at her own disposal, but many of the ships were ancient creaking carcasses, dinosaurs that required a topnotch platoon of mechanics to keep them operational. Not that Oliva minded. She was proud of her resourcefulness and the honest conservation that kept the old vessels humming while, in the command of Anatole Zog, they would have been mothballed years ago.

Oliva was en route from Omega when the President's ship intercepted her just off Delta 3002. The communique the messenger handed her contained the President's red seal, overlaid in gold. The gold slash mean top secret.

The First Fleet was to rendezvous with Earth Station 1, on August 27th. The command to deploy the fleet at Earth Station 1 was not surprising. The First Fleet regularly switched command headquarters between Earth and the Old Colonies. The secrecy itself was only mildly brow-raising. Certain politicians enjoyed turning routine exercises into more glamorous covert operations. It was the last part of the message that caused Oliva to leave the bridge and take a long walk around the upper deck:

You will rendezvous with the Second and Territorial Fleets and await our orders.

"Deirdre, I was hoping to catch you before you retired for the night." Jaffey stepped across the threshold of the animal sanctuary where Deirdre cradled a large wicker basket in her arms. "What's that?"

Deirdre, instead of answering, opened the basket to reveal a writhing nest of vipers. As Jaffey looked on in horror, the snakes began to crawl out of the basket and up Deirdre's forearms, covering them in thick, tortuous bangles. She held her arms out for Jaffey's inspection.

"Touch them, Jaffey," she invited. "They're really quite warm. They aren't at all slimy as you might expect them to be."

"No, thank you." Jaffey retreated, holding her hands up.

Deirdre coaxed the snakes back into the basket and tucked it into the warm straw. She placed a saucer of milk nearby. "They occasionally come out for a drink at night," she said.

"I need to talk to you about Antiquity," said Jaffey easily as they walked toward the ocean. "She's told me a rather preposterous story."

"About the neutrino counter?"

Jaffey's eyes searched Deirdre's face. "Has she told many people?"

"No," said Deirdre quickly. "Nadril, Morgan, Delphi, now you. Besides SOLCOM command, just we few friends."

"And what do the others think?" Jaffey probed. "Her friends, I mean." She held out a hand to help Deirdre over a rock pile.

Deirdre seemed not to have noticed the outstretched hand. She clambered over the rocks unaided. "They don't know what to think," she said reluctantly. "They're confused."

"They don't believe her."

Deirdre hesitated. "They find it difficult."

Jaffey nodded. "I wonder if Antiquity is having a

mental lapse of some sort. Tonight she tried to show me a model of the Near System she's working on. It's something entirely familiar to her but she was quite mixed up in places."

"She's preoccupied sometimes," said Deirdre shortly. "She forgets. We all do."

"She forgot your name tonight," said Jaffey mildly. She stood for a moment looking out over the water. "What about you, Deirdre? Do you believe what she says?"

Deirdre stared hard at Jaffey, then looked away. "I don't know," she said, defeated. "I don't have the data to support or refute her claims."

"Antiquity says the coats of your creatures have thickened prematurely. She cites this as evidence for her theory."

"It's a very imprecise sign," said Deirdre reluctantly. "It's inconsistent and impossible to evaluate in the short term." She looked bitter. "Antiquity has given many years of splendid service. She deserves to be treated seriously, no matter how far-fetched her ideas seem."

"Of course," said Jaffey, chastened.

"Antiquity says you'll be doing the review at SOLCOM," Deirdre said. "I know you'll do a thorough appraisal."

"You can be absolutely confident about that."

There was an uncomfortable pause. Deirdre spoke first. "I forgot to congratulate you on your election," she said clearly. "It must please you very much to be Chief Engineer and a member of the Council at your age. I hear you're the youngest counselor in the history of the Union."

"Yes, I understand that's so." Jaffey paused once

again to look out over the ocean, stopping Deirdre with a touch to the forearm. "Look at this. The water is so still the moonbeam is quite perpendicular.

After a long silence, Jaffey said, "We used to like to walk by the ocean."

"Yes, I remember," Deirdre said quietly.

"We would hold hands." Jaffey's hand closed around Deirdre's.

"Yes." Her voice was low but angry. Jaffey seemed not to notice.

"It was so sweet. You were so shy and so eager."

"I was only sixteen."

"Your body was so white against the pale sand," Jaffey murmured. "And I was windburned — my hair bleached white — from sailing all summer in the South Seas. We couldn't get enough of each other. I wanted to take you to the far corners of the universe, make love to you on a distant star."

"Yes," said Deirdre tensely. "I remember you saying those very words. You were always a romantic, Jaffey. You always said such extravagant things."

"I meant them."

"And the next holiday you came home in your new Space Academy uniform with Tristan at your side," Deirdre said evenly.

Jaffey grimaced. "I was very young and foolish. Tristan was an upperclassman. She seemed so exciting, so handsome in her uniform with all the gold braid and bars of rank. A twenty-year-old head is easily turned."

"So it seems."

Jaffey stared past Deirdre at the water. "How did

I let you get away," she murmured. "I often wondered what life would have been for you if you had gone away to school with me instead of seeking out wizened old hermits as mentors. Living in damp, dreary caves for years on end with nothing but snakes and bats as companions — you'd have received a splendid education on Zeta Base, in vastly improved surroundings."

"I chose the caves as a field of study, not as a convent. I happen to like caves. Besides, someone had to stay near Antiquity. You had left. She and Morgan fought."

Jaffey ignored the message. "We could have had such good times together," she said. "That summer could have gone on forever."

"But it didn't," said Deirdre stiffly. "It's over. It's past. We can be friends again — the way we were when we were children. Sisters."

"Friends, sisters," said Jaffey softly. "Would you have me believe you feel none of the passion you felt that summer on the beach?"

"No. It's gone. Forgotten."

Jaffey looked deep into Deirdre's eyes, making no attempt to hide the passion in her own. "Your eyes say you're lying." She drew Deirdre to her, kissed her lightly on the lips, lingered then backed away. "Your eyes don't know how to lie," she whispered. "Neither do your lips."

For a long moment Deirdre held Jaffey's gaze, defiant, unwavering. Then she looked away. "Good night, Jaffey," she said coolly.

Chapter 4

Marcus Vinkle himself was on hand to lead Jaffey and Millgrew on the tour of SOLCOM.

Well aware of Marcus's glibness and his reputation of being something of a sycophant, Jaffey fell into conversation with Marcus quickly and easily. He was uncommonly bright and devoted to his career, and that was all Jaffey felt she could reasonably expect of a subordinate. She stayed at Marcus's elbow patiently throughout the inspection, impervious to his tendency to direct all conversations into her ear in a very loud voice. Millgrew lingered several feet behind them, repelled less by Marcus's social ineptitude than by his habit of creating minor electrical accidents.

"The equipment is as old as the hills," Marcus told Jaffey, "but it's still as reliable as any of the stuff in the rest of the galaxy." He added with a huge grin, "Takes a whole corps of engineers to keep her humming of course. We're forever rerouting at least one part of the system for repairs. We've had as many as ten shutdowns at a time."

"What is the tolerance of the system?" Jaffey knew the answer, but considered it only proper to let an engineer expand on his own system.

"Tolerance is defined at twelve," said Marcus. "Within rigorous specs, of course. Outside the code, we could probably handle fifteen."

"Wobbly at sixteen?" asked Jaffey.

"Very unstable," said Marcus. He was serious for a moment, then erupted in a huge guffaw. "Explodes at seventeen," he chortled. He glanced up to see Millgrew staring at him, furious. He whispered apologetically to Jaffey, "Sorry. I had forgotten that she was involved in the Volteren explosion. They say it was scary."

"She lost her hair for the better part of a year," Jaffey muttered. "Her left arm was burned quite savagely. She was rather cavalier about the arm but most humiliated about the hair."

Marcus glanced at Millgrew who was standing stiffly, her hands clasped behind her back — a posture that reeked of moral rectitude. Marcus laughed again. Jaffey hushed him with a question:

"The code calls for daily checks, including verifications from auxiliary modems. Is this done according to the book?"

"Most definitely," said Marcus. "We might give the empty nod to some of the minor verifications but never to the daily lists. It's a critical operation, top priority."

"Is this the first time a check has been requested?" Jaffey asked. "I mean, outside the routine annual?"

"No. Usually it's the press, though, looking for a bit of exposé journalism. Or the request comes from one of the outer colonies. Some of the little ones resent having all of their solar intelligence routed through SOLCOM. Little dog mentality. Am I right? One of the little dogs wants a teardown and the President has to respond with an authorization. Political pressure." He looked at Jaffey and winked. "Am I right?"

Jaffey nodded.

"But this time the pressure came from a local source," Marcus continued. "From Jordan Thyme. Antiquity."

"Oh, I thought the request had come through the President," said Jaffey innocently. "I didn't realize Antiquity had approached you personally."

"Oh, yes," said Marcus ruefully. "She's forwarded several formal requests for a check. I felt they weren't justified so I denied them." He shrugged. "What could I do, Jaffey? In each case she had based her request on readings from the ancient neutrino device. How could I recommend a teardown on that basis? I forwarded a copy of the requests and my reasons in each case. The President upheld

60

me the first half-dozen times. But, in the end, what could she do?"

"Antiquity is science-philosopher and Counsel to the Union Exemplar," said Jaffey amicably. "Her experience alone demands the courtesy."

Marcus threw up his arms in surrender. "What's a poor engineer to do?" he cried in mock dismay. "I'm up to my ass in diodes and it seems I have to master the arts of courtesy and politics to boot."

"Don't forget, Marcus," said Jaffey good-naturedly, "you're talking to a politician. Perhaps politics is not a bad skill to master."

"Oh, yes, I heard you had entered politics." Marcus laughed, once again buoyant. "When I heard you had been elected to the Council, I had to chuckle. The chief engineer, a politician! I couldn't believe our good fortune. Too bad your post is minor. Still —" He smiled, then said with a broad wink, "I know a nice-looking blonde in charge of Energy Operations. I'll introduce you to her on the promise of a new direction coordinator."

"What a bad example to set! To bribe me on my first journey! Besides, Therese is a very good friend of mine. She would be quite disgusted with you, Marcus."

"Everyone is disgusted with me," said Marcus with a sigh. "Especially Therese. She has said so many times."

At the technician's signal, each person in the room put on headgear designed not merely to receive audio input, but to feed information directly from the consoles into the human brain.

Jaffey touched her index finger gently to her temple as she prepared to receive the information

61

from the console. The gesture was meaningless but it satisfied, psychologists said, some ancient human need for control.

The technician slid the lever under his right hand full ahead. Jaffey's head was flooded immediately with a dizzying array of patterns, formulae and charts. The technician glanced at Jaffey quizzically. Jaffey smiled and shook her head, but Marcus drew an arm across his forehead in an exaggerated gesture of duress.

Within two hours, the preliminary examination was complete save for the important solar communicator.

"The watchdog of the sun," said Marcus with a grin. "The heart of SOLCOM." He stepped to one side, gesturing Jaffey grandly toward the entrance. "I saved it for last. It seems only appropriate."

A lone technician stood up quickly as they entered, wiping his hands on his pant legs. He nodded to Marcus and left the room. Jaffey stepped across the threshold and paused.

"It's like entering a cathedral," said Marcus. "Makes you want to take your hat off — if you had one, that is." His voice sounded inappropriately loud.

Jaffey nodded. She had been inside the solar communications room many times but she felt the same sense of awe each time, the awe she had felt as a small girl when Antiquity had brought her there for the first time.

The far wall was a solid bank of the latest in monitors, receptors and computer hardware. The floor, however, and the remaining walls were densely black and shimmering like moonlight on an intensely black ocean. The material was quag, the compacted fossil remains of great prehistoric clams discovered four hundred years before in the ocean rift off the Southern Archipelago.

"Needs a paint job," said Marcus unpiously. He let out a hoot that echoed incongruously in the translucent amber dome. For a moment, the sound hung, rung around the dome like a copper medallion spun against hardwood. Then it disappeared, drawn to the pinnacle and extinguished.

"Shh!" said Jaffey. Her eyes were riveted to the great globe that sat on a platform at the center of the floor. The globe was a representation of the ancient sun, set in a ring of mahogany, inlaid with jade and mother-of-pearl and richly carved with primitive representations of sun goddesses, devils, snakes and vultures. Tiny ocher lights flickered over the surface while at the center a red light blinked hypnotically. Jaffey stepped to the platform and stood directly over the gyro.

"It's a relic," said Marcus cheerfully. "A real beaut. Gives me the creeps sometimes, though. Seems out of place, unscientific." He paused. "We should have moved the hardware to a new communications room long ago. Antiquity wouldn't hear of it, of course."

"Review the setup, please," said Jaffey, mesmerized by the globe.

Marcus sighed like a precocious schoolboy called upon to recite an elementary table. "The receiver takes its input from the external 'dish,' as does every monitoring system from the Saturn Rings to the seismology of the fault line of the Great Rift. The input is run through the computer banks. The signals are interpreted, synthesized, recorded and the whole shebang sent out along the line to every scientific station and research lab in the galaxy."

"Backup?"

"There's feed to the auxiliary room next door plus a small monitor in the rear of my office," said Marcus with a shrug. "Same stuff — receive, interpret, transmit. All use the same receptor and transmitter site. The interpret function is slower." Marcus stopped with a sudden laugh. "Mine's as slow as a snail on Pluto but what can you expect from a homemade job?"

Jaffey stared thoughtfully at the computer bank. "You've checked the system personally?"

"Of course." Marcus shrugged. "We found minor static, most likely from component wear."

"Why haven't they been replaced?"

Marcus shrugged again. "Decisions at Supply. Or should I say indecisions. They're not sure if they want to replace or design entirely new components. In the meantime, we're left without a sparker."

"Have you tried grafilm?" asked Jaffey. "We had great success with it in the reception fields on Eosine. The ionic interference there is fierce."

"Yes, we tried grafilm." Marcus glanced about, clicking his tongue. "Spit works better. Sometimes, earwax." He followed with a loud guffaw.

Jaffey laughed and glanced at Millgrew who had just moved to the edge of the platform. To her surprise, Millgrew appeared to be smiling — a very economical smile, to be sure, small and compact and tightly controlled, but a smile nevertheless. There was, at the same time, a tiny dot of astonishment in her pupils, as if she were amazed at her own reaction.

Jaffey turned to Marcus, suppressing a smile. "Shall we run through the check again?"

Marcus didn't bother to summon a technician but went straight to the console and punched in the test sequence himself. He looked to Millgrew, eyebrows raised quizzically. "Ready?"

Millgrew didn't respond. She was wiping fussily at a fine, brown dust on the control panel.

"What's that?" asked Jaffey.

Marcus was concentrating on the monitor. "Oh, it's the backup tape," he said carelessly. "We record the incoming signals for the archives. Gives the theorists something to mull over, you know."

"It looks like crumbs," said Jaffey, surprised.

"Oh, that." Marcus shook his head with annoyance. "Gerald, the technician who operates the recorder, likes to sneak snacks on duty. He has a friend in Central Transcontinenta who makes his own bread. It's awful stuff. Makes a terrible mess. I'm forever calling him up on the carpet over it."

Millgrew had finished sweeping the debris into her handkerchief. She tucked the cloth into her pocket and nodded.

For twenty minutes, there was no sound in the room save for the noise of the equipment. Finally, the lights on the test circuit blinked and dimmed, one by one.

A long silence followed, during which Jaffey and Millgrew seemed lost in thought. Marcus looked from one to the other expectantly.

Jaffey glanced at Millgrew. "I have no choice but to go to teardown," she said reluctantly. "Nothing obvious is wrong and anything less thorough is bound to be unsatisfactory."

Marcus grimaced. "What's a poor engineer to do? Just let me know what you need and when. I'll provide you with all the technical support necessary. We'll commence the switch to auxiliary directly." He said ruefully, "I don't know why I should be surprised. We both knew a teardown would be necessary. What else would satisfy Antiquity?"

"Nothing." Jaffey said. "We'll start tomorrow if that's agreeable to you."

"It'll be touch and go but I think we can make it."

"Good." Jaffey gave Marcus a cheerful pat on the shoulder. "We won't need any support staff. Millgrew and I will muddle through. You'll need all the hands at your disposal, getting the chinks worked out of the auxiliary."

Marcus glanced toward Millgrew who looked prepared to spit. She was not known for her fondness for manual tasks. Marcus's eyes grew wide with amusement and he laughed out loud. "You haven't been in government long enough, Jaffey," he said. "You haven't learned to delegate."

"We're egalitarian at home," said Jaffey pleasantly. "Ours is a small planet. Our people are used to doing things for themselves. They wouldn't know what to do with servants."

"You Zetonians are *so* self-righteous," he chortled. "Pioneers are always egalitarian. Fresh, without original sin. Wait until you are as old as we are. Wait until you've raped a planet."

"Perhaps we'll always be fresh and innocent."

"Hope so." Marcus stepped down from the platform with an exaggerated sigh. "I'm going to have to work like a dog, but I'll have the specs, with the problem delineated, ready for you tomorrow. Eight, sharp." Marcus paused to let Jaffey pass through the door ahead of him. "And if you're free tonight," he added, "I have a block of tickets for the matches. Company box."

"That's very generous. You could have sold them for profit."

Marcus winked. "You know that's illegal," he said. "Tonight, then. I'm looking forward to it. I'll meet you in the mezzanine for drinks, perhaps?"

"Very good, Marcus. Thank you."

The door closed. Jaffey turned at once to Millgrew. "I'm sorry we have to go to teardown," she said. "Politics."

"Yes." Millgrew paused. "I must say, I find the static rather excessive."

Jaffey shrugged. "Ordinary receptor static, I think. The scourge of the universe."

"I thought it rather fine for radio static," Millgrew murmured. "Something else perhaps. Something in the internal assembly. Fine lint perhaps."

"Perhaps?"

"Or dust."

"Impossible!" Jaffey started to laugh. "How could there possibly be dust in the system? It's protected by three air seals."

Millgrew turned away, injured. "These things happen," she said stiffly. "Leaks have been known to occur in the tightest systems."

* * * * *

Marcus went into his office, slamming the door shut behind him. His assistant entered without knocking. Marcus bawled him out and shoved him out of the office, locking the door after him. He sank into his desk chair.

He seldom allowed himself to be the bully, and then only with the lowest of the underlings and always in private. It was such a relief to be assertive! He got so tired of playing the buffoon, a role he had picked up in grade school when he found playing the clown earned him the acceptance his physical appearance denied him.

He stared at the screen in front of him, then flipped the channel to call up a picture of Ludmilla, the foster mother who had taken him in when his biological parents rejected him. Ludmilla, who had loved him in her own peculiar way, who had seen to his superb education. Tears came to his eyes, dripping down his freckled cheeks. She was gone. How he had loved her! He wiped his sleeve across his eyes, his expression suddenly hardening. How he hated her! Hated her for letting him remain ugly, for letting him grow up gauche, unschooled in the social niceties. She had been so pleased with her little freckled-faced, red-headed, jug-eared boy. Later on, when he was old enough to request the necessary surgery on his own, he was too proud to admit his ugliness disturbed him.

Ludmilla! Antiquity! These two old women had ruined his life. He was tired of their dominance, infuriated by what they had done to him. He erased Ludmilla's pictures with guilty pleasure.

He switched the channel to SOLCOM feed and watched it for a moment, tense and unsmiling. When

68

he had finished he applied his personal seal to block the channel from prying eyes and signed off. Vengeance, vindication! His victory was yet to come.

Jaffey watched Deirdre surreptitiously, all the time pretending to be absorbed by the activities of Morgan Quade who was at the match courtside with her camera, the press badge displayed prominently on the pocket of her fatigues stating she was on official business.

Marcus caught Jaffey looking in Morgan's direction. "Does she interest you?"

Jaffey looked at Marcus, momentarily startled. "No, I'm just surprised to see her on such a routine assignment. I would think her editor would be embarrassed to ask."

"She loves earth-gravity sports." Marcus added behind his hand, "Especially if women are involved. I understand she is well-known to at least half of the Academy's rugger team."

Jaffey gave Marcus a cool stare then looked away. She tried to distract herself from Deirdre by searching the stands for Antiquity.

The old woman was not there. Jaffey imagined she was watching a holograph of the matches at home which was, to all intents and purposes, like being at courtside at that moment.

Perhaps, thought Jaffey with a smile, Antiquity had elected to focus on her, Jaffey, her favorite pupil and nominal daughter. If so, she might have noticed she had been observing Deirdre. Perhaps she was scowling.

Jaffey told herself it was selfish of Antiquity to be so possessive of Deirdre. Nevertheless, she squinted and pretended to be absorbed by the quarter-gravity match being shown on the giant screen just over Deirdre's head. In quarter-gravity tennis, it was impossible to follow the movement of the players or the ball with any precision. The players and the ball were tagged with special homing devices that showed up on the screen as bright, rapidly moving dots. The result was like watching a Ping Pong match at exaggerated speed. Those inclined toward intellectualism tended to find quarter-gravity matches stimulating. Jaffey found them hard on the eyes.

Jaffey continued to observe Deirdre. Marcus noticed her distraction.

"Oh, it's the animal person you're interested in," he said with a giggle. "Well, there's no point in looking at her." He leaned toward Jaffey and said in an earnest whisper, "You have that aura of being obsessive, Jaffey. That's not good. It's bad for your soul and with someone like Antiquity, it's bad for your career."

"Why would Antiquity hurt me," Jaffey scoffed. "She's my patron. She would hardly jeopardize my career."

Marcus smiled grimly. "She's getting older," he said. "Old people do strange, unpredictable things."

"Antiquity's my friend," Jaffey said firmly.

Marcus pondered this for a moment then, with a nod toward Morgan, added slyly, "Antiquity acts as if she owns the animal person. And what she doesn't control belongs to Morgan Quade."

Jaffey turned to Marcus, her face crimson. "What do you mean by that?" she asked, her voice strained.

"I mean they're lovers," said Marcus, eager to share some news. "They have been since the animal person returned from the caves in November. Why, it's the talk of our little enclave here. Don't you get any of the good gossip in the Middles, Jaffey?"

"I haven't heard a thing about it," said Jaffey hotly. "Are they declared?"

"No need to declare," Marcus chortled. "They leave the lights on — if you know what I mean." He broke out in a loud guffaw.

"I remember now," Millgrew announced as they were settling for the night. She raised one eyebrow. She looked as intellectually imposing as was possible for one wearing a paisley nightshirt that ended two inches above the knee. "I've heard that particular static before," she announced.

They were quartered in the Grand Hotel, the huge, old-fashioned edifice traditionally set aside for visiting delegates. Normally, a Union representative would have secured the penthouse suite or, at the very least, a group of rooms overlooking the ocean from an upper floor. Millgrew had made the arrangements, however, and, with her penchant for penny-pinching, had requested ordinary convention facilities — shared accommodation to boot.

Jaffey had just taken out her oralizer when Millgrew made her announcement. The device, which cleaned and polished the teeth while removing incipient cavities, had to remain in place at least two minutes.

"I recall hearing it at the same frequency while we were checking the SOLCOM feed on Delta 3002."

Jaffey shrugged. "Well, I guess that makes sense. Delta 3002 receives its signal directly from SOLCOM, static and all."

"But that proves the static is not receptor static," Millgrew persisted. "If it were receptor static the interpreter would recognize it and filter it out before transmitting the signal."

"Quite right." Jaffey was having trouble keeping her mind on the conversation. "I'll bet they're in bed together right now," she murmured. "Morgan Quade! I should have known."

"I beg your pardon?"

"I said we have a big job ahead of us," Jaffey said loudly. "We have a lot to do. Who knows? We could be here for a month. Perhaps longer." She paused for a moment then said quietly, "Or however long it takes me —"

"I beg your pardon?"

"I said, I'm sure the Academy will be glad to have you home for awhile." Jaffey gave Millgrew an affectionate pat on the shoulder. "This mission shouldn't be too strenuous. We'll have our evenings free at least. Not like the transport job where we worked day and night. Maybe you'll be able to meet someone."

"I don't know if I want to meet anyone," said Millgrew, embarrassed. She wished Jaffey wouldn't touch her so casually.

Jaffey tossed her towel in the general direction of

the bathroom. "I'm tired," she said with a yawn. "Are you going to bed now, Millgrew?"

"I think I'll read for a few minutes." Millgrew took out her pocket console and retired to a chair in a corner of the room. She scanned the menu briefly, then entered her selection.

"Joad's new science fiction thriller?" asked Jaffey.

Millgrew grimaced. Everyone liked to tease her about her preference for racy futuristic novels. Her colleagues at the Academy had discovered this proclivity when she had carelessly left her console on hold one day in the staff lounge.

Jaffey dropped into bed and pressed a button to dim the light. As an afterthought, she reached for the case that lay on the bedside table and removed a small box with several dials and a thin metal disk no larger than a thumbnail. She placed the disk on her left temple and, by manipulating the dials, programmed the box to record her dreams for the duration of the night — in 3-D and in color with audio, if available.

Watching one's dreams after the fact was definitely not to everyone's taste. The activity had been described, derisively, as the ultimate in honesty and the ultimate in terror. Dream tapes were regarded as the most personal of all property. By law, they were considered part of the human body. To view another's dreams without permission was considered an extreme act of violence. It was, of course, strictly forbidden to use the device to record the waking thoughts of another.

Jaffey said good night to Millgrew and turned off her light. Millgrew did not respond.

Chapter 5

Morgan Quade ushered the cub reporter to the ladder that led down to the gondola. She waited until the woman had climbed halfway down, then followed, slamming the hatch behind her.

The woman stepped from the bottom rung and looked about with a gasp.

She had never been in the gondola before. Few had. The bubble, a transparent globe, crisscrossed with a crude metal grid, had been commissioned for the express use of Morgan Quade. Her editor, indulgent in everything, had succumbed to her desire for a mobile studio resembling a gun turret from the ancient wars. The camera too lent an air of authenticity, centered and angled to mimic the equipment of the legendary tailgunner.

The only oddity was a transparent platform, perhaps ten feet in diameter, in the middle of the floor. Right now, it was centered over the eye of a Martian tornado and reflected in the mirrored ceiling.

Morgan turned to the woman and said, "I want you to take off your clothes."

The reporter stared at Morgan, eyes widening, not from fear but from surprise. "Did I hear you correctly, Morgan?"

"The composition is called 'Vortex,'" Morgan explained quickly. She moved rapidly about the perimeter of the turret, adjusting the cameras, checking the lighting. "I want to shoot you against the funnel of the tornado."

As she spoke, the woman began to undress. Her eyes never left Morgan.

"I want you to lie down in the middle of the platform." Morgan led the woman to the platform, positioned her above the vortex, and arranged the woman's compliant limbs. "You're perfectly free to say no, of course," she said easily.

The platform was pleasantly warm and vibrated gently. The woman looked at Morgan, a trace of a smile on her lips. "But I don't want to say no."

"Good." Morgan looked from her subject to the camera with a practiced eye. "I didn't think you would, otherwise I wouldn't have picked you in the first place."

"Why didn't you say something beforehand?"

"The element of surprise," murmured Morgan. She seemed quite detached. "If you had been prepared in advance, we would have sacrificed the spontaneity." She walked to the edge of the turret and removed her flight suit, then the fatigues. Under the fatigues, she wore nothing but a loincloth tucked into a worn fabric belt. She stood for a moment, staring at the woman. "I'm going to make love to you," she said. "You've probably guessed that by now."

"Yes."

"But only if you are in absolute agreement, of course."

"I am. Absolute."

Morgan knelt over the woman and said into the microphone, "Lower us, please."

The vortex loomed large in the mirror — a greedy, dizzying enchantress. The woman's eyes widened with fright.

"It's all right," Morgan murmured. She spoke softly, her eyes never leaving her companion's. "I wouldn't expose you to danger."

The woman nodded, lips parted. The vortex closed about them, a swirling funnel of orange and yellow, rimmed with charcoal and embedded with flecks of red and elusive sparks of emerald and sapphire. Then the colors blended and swirled together in a glowing white cone.

Morgan's fingers searched and probed, touching flesh, widening the space.

Then came the noise, a low distant rumble, building to an apogee of intense vibration. Morgan covered the woman's body in a thin, hot flame.

Morgan leapt up and pulled on her fatigues. She started to turn away, then paused and tenderly covered the woman with a thick gray blanket. Then, without a word, she scampered up the ladder and ran, barefooted, through the corridor to the cockpit.

The still was fixed on the monitor. The mobile pulsated in the viewfinder, a vibrant writhing of tornado within tornado — throbbing, exploding. Morgan stared at the still, apparently satisfied. "Talent," she said.

A voice crackled over the radio. "All ships in the vicinity of Mars," said the voice of the newsroom dispatcher, "there's been a vapor explosion over the Elysium fields. Who will take? I need two."

Morgan grabbed the receiver. "It's Morgan," she said. "We'll take it."

"Roger," said the dispatcher. "Have you got the equipment?" She was referring to the special headgear necessary to navigate the vapor.

"Check," Morgan lied.

"Fuel?"

"We'll just make it."

Several workers were already dead, vaporized by the explosion. The emergency vessel had taken the last two survivors. Telda Am, the station supervisor, had stayed behind in a fruitless attempt to rescue her vanished companions.

The Elysium fields were a dangerous place to work. Telda had known that before she took the assignment. Some said the fields should never have been developed, but in a fuel-hungry universe, the lure of energy-dense macromite was irresistible — at least to the pirates. And Telda Am was a pirate.

An unfortunate by-product of the mining process was phosphide, a thick, pungent gas that hung in the air and posed a constant threat with its explosive potential. Vapor fumes could be dispelled, but nothing could protect against the unforeseen. Earlier that day, a small asteroid had struck Elysium in a flaming arc, exploding the dense layer of phosphide that hung nearest the surface.

Telda Am had been underground when the initial explosion occurred. She had helped the emergency shuttle evacuate the crew. Now with everyone accounted for, she clung to the top of the control tower, hoping against hope that another emergency vessel would appear, an emergency vessel with the temerity to dive into the flickering embers of a phosphide fire.

Morgan Quade leaned toward the port of the gyrocraft, straining for the first glimpse of the Elysium fire.

Phosphide fires were unlike any other fire. At the surface, they were white hot and sent a dense fog laced with searing embers into the air for meters above the main explosion. From a distance, the fire looked like the twinkling lights of a large settlement. Occasionally, the flares would coalesce to form pockets of burning gas, often large and frequently violently explosive.

Morgan began to tug on her flight suit. She started to put her boots on without socks, then thought better of it. She had done that on Vengus and had been unable to walk for a week.

"If we get too close, we'll set off an explosion," said Shenkel, her co-pilot. His eyes were trained anxiously on the altimeter. "We don't have much to spare, Morgan."

Morgan nodded. Shenkel was braver than he sounded. He was absolutely right about the explosion. She began to pull on her helmet. She didn't have a mask. She disguised that fact by putting an extra-heavy pair of goggles on over the camera and pulling the absorbent layer of her flight suit firmly above her chin. She buckled the suit and fastened the zipper on her left boot. "When I say so, give me ten meters."

Morgan climbed down the ladder, slamming the hatch closed behind her. She fastened the heavy tryphite hook on the hatch door into the webbing of her suit. The outer hatch opened with a touch of the foot. She kicked free, pushing with her arms to make sure that the guidewire was free. She could hear the muffled sounds of the ship, then she was alone.

"Ten meters," she said into the helmet.

The guidewire played out slowly. She was in the middle of a thick gray-white fog. Particles of phosphide caught fire and blazed before her eyes. Half-spent embers sizzled against the cool metal hardware of her flight suit. She took a deep breath and used ten percent of the air trapped within the flight suit.

"Twenty meters," she said quickly.

The guidewire jerked, stopped, then dropped abruptly. Morgan clenched her teeth as the harness cut into her armpits and groin.

Telda Am heard the faint rumble of the gyrocraft

and, looking up, was almost certain she could make out a brace of green tail lights. But it was hopeless. She had lost her two-way radio and had no means of signaling. Besides, she was charred from the explosion and weakened and ill from breathing the poisons that seeped in and around the edges of her damaged filtration mask.

Morgan gulped. Half the air in the suit was gone.

Out to her right, the phosphide embers danced in a dense cloud, attracted to each other as bees to honey. There was a muffled *pop* as the embers coalesced and burst into flames. Morgan took some photographs and turned away.

"Ten meters," she said.

The guidewire inched out slowly. Morgan's foot struck something solid. The guidewire went slack.

Morgan took a shallow breath. She could barely hear the navigator and didn't want to waste her precious air in an effort to reply. The platform she had landed on seemed at least semisolid. However, with the fire flickering below, it was impossible to know how long it would remain secure. She took some pictures and braced herself to push off. A weak but persistent force held her to the platform. She swore softly and reached down to free her boot. She looked directly into the glazed but hopeful eyes of Telda Am. The eyes contained a plea. They also contained thanks. Telda Am knew she would not be left alone to die in an obscure mining camp at the edge of nowhere.

For a moment, Morgan stared, stunned by the

expression on the woman's face. Then she quickly unfastened the guidewire and hooked it into the webbing on Telda's safety harness. Then, in one motion, she leapt up, wrapped the guidewire around her wrist and gave two quick, urgent tugs with her free hand. She took a deep breath and exhausted the air in her suit.

Morgan grasped the woman firmly under the armpits with her free arm and clung grimly to the guidewire. The woman was alive. She could feel the faint, choking respirations against her chest. She grimaced as the guidewire seared her wrist. Her lungs bucked and burned. The woman, now delirious, began to struggle and fight. Morgan held on, her lungs ready to burst. Finally, unable to endure any longer, she wrenched open the stopper on her helmet and breathed the poison air.

A large funnel of phosphide to the right exploded into a plume of angry red flame. The gyrocraft shuddered above them as the guidewire raced the final ten meters.

Morgan's right hand was cruelly abraded as they were jerked unceremoniously through the hatch.

Shenkel slammed his foot to the floor and the vessel shot up like a cork from a bottle of festive brew. The phosphide embers coalesced behind them and exploded in a great white wall of flame.

Morgan hauled down the portable respirator and went to work immediately on Telda Am. Shenkel leaned over the controls, weeping quietly to himself. Then, exhausted, Morgan crawled to the corner behind the navigator's chair and sat there, stunned, the blood from her wrist mixing with the soot and residue and running off her flight suit in a weak, smoky drizzle.

Chapter 6

The teardown of solar receptor number one, SOLCOM main, proceeded laboriously. It was a tedious job, involving small instruments, scanners, audiophones and high-quality magnification. At times, Jaffey's short, thick fingers — however talented — would prove too clumsy for the task. Then Millgrew would take over, her delicate, slender fingers tracing the honeycombed circuitry like a blind person reading the pattern of a spider's web. The level of concentration required for the task was phenomenal. As she always did at such times, Jaffey gave a silent thanks to Antiquity for her grim emphasis on the values of diligence and discipline.

By the end of the tenth day, Jaffey had an enormous headache. She guessed Millgrew was similarly affected. Although Millgrew said nothing, she opted to skip dinner in favor of an energy pill and a dip in the hotel pool.

Jaffey tried to close her eyes and nap, but sleep would not come.

She remembered when her biological parents had come to visit her on Zeta Base. The woman was beautiful and intelligent, the man stocky and blond and cheerful. They seemed pleased with their creation. They gave her tablets containing images of themselves and their personal histories and, also, genealogies. Even as a small girl, it was clear to her she had inherited her mother's mind and her father's physique.

The first meeting of a child and her biological parents was a formal affair, required by law throughout the universe. Subsequent meetings were entirely discretionary. Relationships within the biological family were left free to grow and develop as would any friendship or to wither and die from neglect and indifference. Occasionally — although rarely — the principals detested one another outright. Jaffey, for one, was fond of her biological parents and looked forward to visits and correspondence.

Strong feelings of duty and responsibility, however, were the pleasures of the patrons. Antiquity was the principal patron. Being an influential person she had the privilege of selecting the brightest, most promising young people in the galaxy to be her protégés. In the thirteenth decade of her life she had selected Jaffey, Deirdre and Morgan Quade from a long list of potential stars.

Antiquity must have mixed feelings about her selections, Jaffey thought. She doted on Deirdre who returned her affection without reservation. The old woman, in spite of her protestations to the contrary, loved Morgan intensely. But they had quarreled incessantly since Morgan uttered her first word. Morgan and Antiquity were too much alike, Jaffey thought with a wry smile — soulmates, united yet ripped apart by their stubborn antagonism and arrogant disregard for the opinions of anyone else.

With a sigh, Jaffey folded her arms behind her head. Her feelings for Antiquity weren't quite so straightforward. Although she certainly didn't possess Deirdre's all-consuming devotion, she was fond of the ancient matriarch. She herself was too worldly, too sophisticated to entertain Deirdre's sort of dedication. Zoology was a soft science, riddled with inexactitudes, rife with ancient lore. Deirdre still looked to Antiquity as a mentor in her professional life. Being exposed to new worlds might have changed things. Going away to study had certainly changed things for Jaffey. The professors at the Academy always spoke of Antiquity politely, very often with affection. But Jaffey sensed her new mentors considered Antiquity well past her prime as a scientist. They made little jokes about Antiquity's preference for out-of-date equipment and chuckled over her reliance on hunch and luck in scientific discovery. Jaffey assured herself she had found a respectable middle ground: she valued the strong foundation Antiquity had given her but harbored a healthy skepticism for Antiquity's credentials as a hard scientist.

The dream recorder Jaffey had plugged in suddenly transformed the clear edges of the ceiling into a magical sky of sparkling blues and pinks and yellows. The colors folded upon one another in a soft-edged kaleidoscope, disappeared, then exploded in a shower of shimmering pastels. Jaffey stared at the ceiling, open-mouthed.

Deirdre floated toward her on a billowy pink cloud, draped in gossamer sheaths and dappled with dewdrops. Jaffey watched, breathless. At the corner of the dream, she saw herself, hesitant and red-cheeked and rigid in the uniform of a cadet. Deirdre called out. The words echoed in her head. *Come to me. Come to me.* Jaffey stepped forward tentatively, afraid the rough fabric of her tunic would shred the iridescent splendor. She reached to take her in her arms but Deirdre was staring past her, her lips parted in erotic rapture. Morgan Quade alighted at her side, like a large swooping bird from the heavens. She enfolded Deirdre in her arms and disappeared with her into a puffy pink fog. Jaffey lay on the bed and watched as they made love in the splendid shadows. Her heart pounded.

Without warning, the fairy tale disappeared. She was left alone in her dream, standing at the edge of a desert crater while the sky turned into a sheet of bleak blue metal. A wolf howled in the distance.

The ceiling suddenly went blank. Jaffey reached over to push the OFF button.

The light over the door flickered, and Millgrew entered the room. Her hair stood up on her head in little tufts. Her face was pinched and mildly abraded from the long session in the pool.

Jaffey pointed toward the dream recorder. "I was so close to making love to her," she said, chagrined. "You would hope to have the edge in your own dreams at least."

"I should think so," said Millgrew. Her voice was tight and pinched.

"I'm right for her," said Jaffey, quietly fierce. "I know that. Chief Engineer, Counselor, pilot of my own ship. Think what I could give her. All the things I promised her when we were children. It's all out there, Millgrew," she whispered, her voice tinged with awe. "Endless space, a never-ending Christmas tree hung with stars, sparkling like crystal ornaments." She fell back onto the bed, cupping her hands behind her head with a sigh. "Imagine the pleasure, Millgrew. Imagine the joy of showing it to her, sharing it with her."

"Yes," said Millgrew quickly. "I can imagine."

"Millgrew," said Jaffey impatiently, "you're older, you've had a declared partner. You must have some sense for these romantic adventures."

"I can't help you," said Millgrew. "When I was in school, I was totally absorbed in my studies. Mila took me as a partner while I was still very young. She left. What can I tell you? I'm not particularly sophisticated about these things — nor successful."

"Well at least you can tell me this," said Jaffey. "If you had to choose between me and Morgan Quade, whom would you pick?"

"Why, you of course," said Millgrew, befuddled.
"Why?"

"Because —" Millgrew paused, as if to control her feelings. "Because I know you," she said quickly. "I don't know Morgan Quade. I can't say if I would like her or not."

"You're no help at all," said Jaffey with a sigh. "I'll just have to record again," she told Millgrew. "This time, perhaps I'll have better luck."

Chapter 7

When Antiquity woke the next morning, the faint
fingers of light that spread across the floor from the
small, uncovered window were much longer than
usual. She turned to her bedside table and fiddled
with the dials on the galaxy clock until she could
see the luminous figures clearly. Today, the face was
a hodgepodge of interlocking test patterns. A small
flashing light in the lower right-hand corner told her
there had been a transmission failure during the
night.

For a few minutes Antiquity lay very still, gazing

about the room in a mild daze. The room was starkly white and, save for the bed and table, virtually without furnishings. The clothing she had worn the day before was hidden from view, hung on a thick peg in a small corner closet.

The bed was like the room, virtually untouched, the sheets smooth, the corners mitered as severely as they were when she retired. She wondered at what age old people ceased to move during sleep. She knew that she seldom moved. She wondered if the dreams of the old were deliberately sedate.

Then she heard the sound of a gong emanating faintly from a distant place. It was not the sound of a clock striking the hour or that of a timed siren but a familiar sound that told her, however imprecisely, she was late.

She dressed and went out into her quarters. It was too late to make breakfast. She took an energy pill instead, then poured a glass of water and went out onto the balcony.

There was not a cloud to be seen. The sky was dull blue, reflected on the ocean in faded gray-green. A small flock of herring gulls hovered at the water's edge, waiting expectantly for their morning meal. Deirdre was attempting to introduce the birds into the wild. So far, they remained totally dependent. They were poor hunters and Deirdre was too soft-hearted to ignore their plaintive, hungry cries.

Deirdre was in the nursery, feeding a leguminous pap to an orphaned white-tailed fawn. The fawn would not feed from the mechanical mother and the wet nurse Deirdre used in emergencies had rejected him. Deirdre was left to feed the fawn by hand, a tedious and time-consuming task that made most of the keepers sigh. Deirdre, however, seemed not to mind.

Deirdre's hair was damp and her skin looked very fresh. Antiquity guessed she had been romping with the pachyderms or swimming with the sea otters.

"I'm late," Antiquity said casually. "My alarm failed to function. Did Gottfried disconnect the main box? I know it amuses him, but it's most inconvenient."

Deirdre looked at Antiquity strangely and put the fawn aside. The infant took a few wobbly steps then returned to lie at her side, resting his head against her foot.

"The transmission failure didn't occur last night, Antiquity," she said. "It was the night before. You must have forgotten to adjust your clock."

Antiquity stared, confused and suspicious. For a moment, she felt pure fury. Then she acquiesced, smiling graciously. "Of course," she said meekly. "I have been very busy lately and, at times, preoccupied."

Deirdre looked at her sadly but did not challenge her. She put her hand down to stroke the fawn. "Have you any appointments today, Antiquity?"

"Oh, yes," she said carelessly. "Many."

She flinched inwardly as she said this because, in fact, requests for consultations had begun to dwindle of late. Her staff seemed to have trouble filling time. One staff member had been granted a transfer and had not been replaced. She had been told no one was available with the skills she required. She wanted to believe the official explanation. The alternative was simply too devastating — that a person of her stature should have to bicker over resources and engage in petty political maneuvers to meet basic needs was unconscionable.

She looked down at her hands, hardly daring to breathe. Lately, she had had to make work, initiate proposals, in order to give her department a semblance of purposeful activity. She had told herself that ebb and flow was in the nature of her work. This was, of course, not true. Her department had always been hectic in a most regular way. The recent downturn was very peculiar.

She glanced at Deirdre's clock — it was functioning perfectly — and at Deirdre. She imagined there had been whispers and she wondered if Deirdre had heard them. When had the gossip started? When had the first lapse occurred? Had it been noted officially? Had someone entered it in her file? She thought of these things and felt old and feeble. Then she thought of the neutrino counter and the feelings of impotence turned to pure terror. The fear rose in her throat like bile, clawing at her chest with great unforgiving fingers. She forced the feelings down. There was much to do and very little time to do it. Certainly there was no time to dither and dilute her efforts in fruitless hand-wringing.

She turned to Deirdre and said clearly, "Yes, I have many appointments. I may have to cancel some of them, however. I have an important paper to present to the Academy, Thursday. I have scarcely had an opportunity to work on it." She saw Deirdre's questioning glance and said, "Yes, I have elected to hold my philosophical treatise for another occasion. The Academy has heard enough of that sort of thing. Perhaps at a later date." She looked away, staring at her hands once again. "Yes," she said, "the paper I am preparing is very important." She muttered, as if speaking to herself. "It is really quite urgent."

Deirdre touched her arm and smiled indulgently.

Antiquity looked at her. Deirdre was such a comfort — the best of the lot — better than Morgan who was lost to her and, although she loved her dearly, better than Jaffey who seemed carelessly facile at times and lacking a proper sense of values.

You are a blessing to an old woman, she wanted to say but the words would not come, choked off by years of pride and stubbornness.

Morgan Quade waited in her editor's office to hear her fate. For the past five years, her name had stood perpetually in nomination for the title, Grand Master. Last night, the trustees of the Art Academy had met to consider her application once again. In keeping with custom, several other names had been put forward, but none of those artists was given a chance to succeed. The Trustees had promised a decision by mid-morning. Alf had gone to the Academy offices to receive the news.

Normally, Morgan would have been pacing the office and pestering the technicians unmercifully. Today, however, she sat back in Alf's chair with her feet on Alf's desk and gazed out the window, totally enervated.

Early that morning, she had awakened Deirdre from a sound sleep and had taken her to swim in the water in front of the compound. They had walked naked from their bed, down the steps and along the beach. They entered the water just as the first sliver of light pierced the dense gray horizon. It was, for minutes, an intense orange against charcoal, reflected on the water as a single pure beam. Then, gradually, it shredded, then lightened and diluted until it was possible to see the fresh, iridescent bubbles flow backwards from the beach and in again, riding the crests of the gentle swells.

Morgan stretched out in Alf's chair and closed her eyes.

She and Deirdre stood together in the cold water, barely touching at the fingertips, their nipples bold and erect from the chill. She took Deirdre up onto the beach, onto the wet, hard sand and made love to her. She didn't know whether Antiquity was watching and she didn't care. When she had finished, she led Deirdre back into the water and washed her.

She sat in her editor's chair now, her feet on his desk, wearing a clean suit of khaki fatigues, her body smelling of Deirdre and salty sea water. The flesh near the scars stung as if they remembered the salt and the cold.

Alf walked in and removed his jacket. He sat down in the chair on the opposite side of the desk. Morgan looked at him for a moment, then turned away.

"The answer is no, isn't it?"

He shrugged. "No one was chosen," he said regretfully. "You were, of course, the only candidate seriously considered. The trustees were stunned by your work."

"But not stunned enough to grant the title."

Alf sighed. "Girghis told me, privately, that it is

94

almost impossible to evaluate your work anymore," he said. "It can only be admired."

She leaned toward him, her eyes cold with anger. "I deserve the title."

He looked at her wistfully for a moment, then smiled. "Of course you do. Everyone knows that. Girghis also said you are unlikely to receive the title while Melchior lives. He's a very old man and he takes such pleasure in being the only living Grand Master."

"I am a thousand times more talented than Melchior," she said sullenly. "Look at his stills. Pedestrian in theme and execution."

"Yes," he said. "But, in four or five years, you will be a Grand Master. By that time Melchior will be dead. He has led a most dissolute life."

"It's ridiculous," she said sulkily. "I've poured my very soul into my art. And I'm destined to be held back by a doddering old man with an unmitigated ego."

The editor raised his eyebrows and grimaced helplessly. "To be a Grand Master, Morgan," he said softly, "is just a matter of time. Not a matter of passion but of wisdom and time."

She was scarcely listening to him. She got up and went to the window, shaking her curls loose over the collar of her fatigues. "I want the title now," she said. "I'll go to the ends of the galaxy. I'll create a work so dazzling the public will beat the doors down for my nomination. They could hardly refuse me then, in spite of Melchior's vanity."

"No," he acknowledged. "If the public demanded it, they could not."

"Ask Shenkel to bring me the weather charts,"

she said abruptly. "There's a gas fire in the Lazarus Marsh."

He looked at her for a long moment. "No."

She stared out the window, undaunted. "I'll pay for the trip myself if the paper is unwilling," she said. She pressed against the pane, her eyes darting over the passageways below. "You've always let me go overbudget before," she added sullenly. "You've always said what's good for Morgan Quade is good for the paper."

"But not necessarily good for *you*." He added quickly, "I've received your post-flight health review, Morgan." He reached into the basket on his desk, took out a small disk no larger than a silver dollar, and inserted it into his console. "Ruptured left eardrum for the eleventh time. Right has already been ruptured more times than anyone would care to count. Labyrinthitis, requiring electroplacement. Very painful procedure. Excess torque reopened old scars in both kidneys. You need another lung replacement. The scans indicate you have spontaneous bleeding and painful episodes of dyspnea. That little side trip into Elysium didn't help."

She shrugged.

"You were gassed," he concluded. "You forgot your vapor mask and you wouldn't wait to have it delivered."

"The artistic moment doesn't wait for the delivery of errant gas masks," she said sarcastically.

"That's too bad," he said, "because you're suspended. Bellamy will pick up your assignments." He said the words quickly, as if he didn't want to say them. "You're grounded. No more flights until you have medical clearance."

She laughed. "So, I'll get Shenkel to take me up on his off-duty time. He has a ship and he can be bought."

"If Shenkel takes you up, he'll never fly again," he said, his face suddenly pale. "I'll see to it personally. You're grounded pending resolution of the medical problems cited in this report. I've already notified the airport."

"The medical problems cited in this report," she mimicked.

"They must be attended to," he repeated. He turned the console off and took out the disk with an air of finality.

"When can I fly again?"

"When you have a clean bill of health. Two weeks, at least. You need the rest." He folded his arms across his chest. "If it takes longer than two weeks, so be it."

She looked at him, her lips curling into a sardonic smile. "You're enjoying this, aren't you?"

"No," he said quietly, "I'm not. We need your photographs. Your layoff is a burden to everyone. I do have an assignment for you."

She looked at him without interest.

"Jaffey's doing a teardown at SOLCOM," he said. He reached into his pocket and took out a plate of disks. "Here's the background information."

"Grade-three science," she sniffed.

"Write it for the kids then," he said with a smile. "Choose whatever angle suits you. Hang around the legislature. Find out what the politicos think. What do the bureaucrats want? Are we going to a new system? Can we afford it? You know, that sort of thing."

"Politics is Jen's beat," she said sullenly.

"So, you're doing a special feature," he coaxed. "A sidebar. Whatever you do, it will be good. I don't care as long as it keeps you busy. I shudder to think what you could do to yourself with time on your hands."

She picked up her camera bag and started toward the door. "Maybe I'll go to the launch pad and inhale the exhaust. If I'm lucky, I might catch a bit of carbon."

Jaffey lay on her back, squinting through the viewfinder while her fingers manipulated the microtools. Millgrew knelt, hunched over beside her, operating the sonar tap, her ear tuned keenly to the sharp electronic echo. Millgrew seemed distracted and aggrieved, but Jaffey was so engrossed in her work that she failed to notice the high-topped boot or the toe that nudged her repeatedly in the buttock.

"They told me I might find a couple of grease monkeys here," said Morgan, the camera bag slung carelessly over her right shoulder.

Jaffey slid out from under the console at once. Millgrew straightened with a groan and removed her earpiece.

"Press," said Morgan briskly. She flipped her lapel to show her pass. "You're tearing down SOLCOM. What's the story?"

Jaffey pointed toward a pile of discarded coffee cups. "Mostly garbage." She wiped her hand on her coveralls and offered it to Morgan. "Marcus told me you would be covering the story. SOLCOM must be a crashing bore after the Elysium fields."

"I'm grounded," said Morgan bitterly. "I've been assigned to SOLCOM to keep me out of trouble." She sat down on the desk. "So, tell me the story."

"A good teardown has therapeutic as well as diagnostic value," Jaffey said.

"According to my sources, SOLCOM's figures are right on. Why fix what isn't broken?" Morgan folded her arms, mildly disdainful.

Jaffey glanced around. One of the technicians was eyeing them curiously. "I'm just about to take a break," she said. "Why don't you come with me?" Jaffey tossed her gloves aside and led Morgan down the hall. "The gym's very private," she said when they were alone. She started to take off her clothes.

Morgan hauled out a memo screen from her hip pocket. "SOLCOM had an internal review less than two months ago," she said, glancing at her notes. "The system was pronounced one hundred percent fit. Now you're doing, not only a review, but an expensive full-scale teardown. Why?"

Jaffey had stripped down to her underwear. She turned to the tub of resin and sunk her arms in to the elbows. "You've done your homework," she said.

"Let me tell you why SOLCOM is doing the teardown," Morgan said caustically. She snapped the notebook shut and put it in her pocket. "Antiquity has a bee in her bonnet. This ancient piece of glass and metal she so generously calls a neutrino counter tells her the sun is losing power. She sticks to this belief in spite of the fact that a vastly more sophisticated system tells her otherwise. Antiquity starts sending out alarms, first to SOLCOM command and finally to the President herself. A teardown is expensive. The President and Marcus hold Antiquity at bay as long as possible. Finally, bored by Antiquity's persistence and a little bit afraid that her bizarre story could create panic and economic dislocations, they agree to do a teardown. They're doing this to silence Antiquity. Period."

Jaffey did several chin-ups before responding. "Obviously Antiquity has confided in you."

"Yes, again and again," she said. "If she possessed less soul I would say she was a silly old woman. I would say she was insane except insanity seems a heavy burden outside the artistic community." She crossed her arms. "Don't get me wrong, Jaffey. There's nothing saccharine about my feelings for Antiquity. We barely tolerate each other." She paused to arrest the edge of emotion that had crept into her voice. "Let's just say we understand each other."

Jaffey leapt to the rope and climbed nimbly to the top. "Are you saying you believe her? You doubt SOLCOM's readings?"

Morgan shook her head. "The technology is laborious. It defies the comprehension of even a sophisticated layperson like myself, but I have a problem with the concept of infallibility."

Jaffey slid down the rope, landing in front of Morgan with a soft thud. "The scuttlebutt," she said quietly, "is that Antiquity has suffered some mental instability of late. Memory lapses and the like. There are notations in her security dossier. There was even some talk about lifting her security clearance but the President refused to sign the papers." She looked hard at Morgan. "This is confidential. We've agreed — the President, SOLCOM command, myself — to keep Antiquity's name out of this debacle. We'd like the press to cooperate too."

Morgan shrugged. "The President wants to save the old woman any embarrassment. Very sweet of her. Why shouldn't I go along?"

"That's good," said Jaffey. "There's nothing to be gained by making Antiquity look foolish."

"Nothing but journalistic integrity." Morgan gave a wry smile and raised a hand as Jaffey started to object. "Save your arguments for the constitutionalists. You don't have to convince me. I'm an artist. The only reality that matters is mine. And, if you want to keep your tail from being singed in a volcano, you learn to be nimble." She looked at Jaffey and said impishly, "Want to wrestle?"

"Why not?"

They stared at one another, unsmiling, then undressed. Jaffey took off her chronometer and class ring and placed them with her clothes on the bench. Morgan removed the metal band from her wrist. She hesitated over the solid gold band, then removed it too.

"Life in the Middle Colonies must agree with you," said Morgan dryly. "Too many peeled grapes perhaps."

Jaffey merely smiled. They knelt together on the mat, shoulders touching. "You'll find I'm in excellent shape," Jaffey said. "I work out daily."

"I hear your most strenuous workouts occur at night." Morgan clenched her teeth, straining against Jaffey's solid torso.

"Gossip," said Jaffey. She turned quickly, pinning

Morgan under her. "Everyone likes to gossip about the department heads."

"I understand it's more than gossip," said Morgan. She groaned as she strained against Jaffey's weight.

"I don't photograph mine, Morgan Quade."

"Mine is art," said Morgan between clenched teeth, "not a roll in the hay at every port." She moved suddenly, like a snake beneath Jaffey and pinned her to the mat, prone.

"I'm a young woman," said Jaffey, breathless. She winced as Morgan tightened the grip on her wrist. "I have a healthy appetite. Even one as austere as Antiquity wouldn't fault me for that."

"You could always get away with anything with Antiquity," hissed Morgan. "You were always her favorite." Jaffey's body felt cool and silky beneath her. She relaxed her grip for a moment, stunned by its sensuality.

Jaffey reacted instantly. She twisted out of Morgan's grasp and slid Morgan under her. "Nonsense. She gave you far more leeway than she gave any other protégé." Jaffey strained to hold Morgan under her. "Even when you rebelled and ignored her guidelines, she was forgiving."

"And you were so good," Morgan challenged. "Always so obliging, so polite in your dealings with the elders."

"They don't give out medals for stubbornness."

They had stopped struggling. For how long they didn't know. They lay facing each other, staring into each other's eyes. Their bodies softened, melted into each other.

Suddenly Morgan turned violently, throwing

Jaffey roughly to the mat. She straddled her, crushing into Jaffey's buttock.

"If Deirdre were here she would beg us to stop," said Jaffey, gasping. "Remember how she always cried when we fought."

"Deirdre can't stand pain in others," hissed Morgan. "Fortunately she isn't here." She pinned Jaffey's arm to her shoulder blade. Jaffey grasped Morgan by the shoulder and threw her over her head to the mat. She was on her in a flash, straddling her and pinning both arms.

"I want her," she said almost in a whisper. She lowered herself over Morgan so she was speaking inches from her face.

"I want her too."

Jaffey tightened her grip. "You have nothing to offer," she growled. "I'll be President one day. I can give her the universe. You've kept her small and brown and plain — like one of her little sparrows. You're as bad as Antiquity, hiding her away to satisfy your needs when you return from your escapades. A mistress. A slavegirl." She stared into Morgan's eyes. "You like that, don't you? You're a barbarian, a vandal. Deirdre should have status, recognition, adulation —"

Morgan's eyes bored into Jaffey's. "You underestimate her. You would make her a bauble," she accused. "Something to wear on your arm like your precious chevrons."

Jaffey reddened. "Not a bauble," she protested. "A star."

She pressed forward slightly. Their nipples brushed. For a time the room was perfectly still.

Suddenly a voice crackled from the intercom.

"Morgan Quade," it said, "Dr. Norbert has been trying to locate you to remind you you are late for your appointment."

Jaffey relaxed her grip and Morgan wriggled free. She grabbed her clothes. Jaffey watched for a moment, then rose and picked up her own clothes.

"When we were children, we fought for her," she called after Morgan. "We pretended we were knights in the court of the legendary Arthur. Antiquity was Merlin and Deirdre was the beautiful Guinevere."

"We aren't children anymore," Morgan said. She slid the gold band onto her finger and left the room.

Morgan Quade's body was a patchwork of scars — old burns, lacerations and abrasions. The scanner detected each one and recorded it on the oscilloscope as a three-dimensional blip that indicated size, type and absolute thickness. The blips were also color-coded. Most of them showed up on the screen as a bright, lively blue. Two, tracking a pair of small, deep lacerations on the left thigh, glowed red. Delphi Norbert shook her head. She passed the scanner over the red areas once again, then turned it off with a decisive click.

"The lesions on your thigh are cancerous," she said. "We'll have to sound them."

"It will take forever," said Morgan petulantly. "I'm already getting restless. Besides, I have an appointment."

"Nonsense," said Delphi cheerfully. "It won't take more than a minute." She removed the depth sound from its case, then positioned the viewfinder over

Morgan's thigh. She said to Morgan with a smile, "Ready?"

"It'll hurt," said Morgan sullenly.

Delphi shook her head. "Oh, Morgan," she said cheerfully, "it doesn't hurt at all. It barely tickles. Besides, you're immune to pain. Isn't that what you always say?" She squinted into the viewfinder. "You haven't been wearing the proper goggles either. I'll need to examine your eyes again in a week," she added grimly. "It's a shame someone with your vitality, your —"

"Rawness?"

"Yes, that's a good word. It's a shame you court death so assiduously. You have a brilliant mind. You're respected — revered by some. The universe is at your fingertips. You should be preparing for your role as a patron. At the very least, you should consider your responsibility to the gene pool."

Morgan made a face. "I don't want to be a parent."

"Of course you do," said Delphi soothingly. "I could harvest an egg right now. The scanner shows you're ovulating."

"I have no desire to have my eggs sloshing around in a bowl with some degenerate sperm," said Morgan. "Harvest my eggs indeed," she muttered. "Here I am, reduced to the level of one of Deirdre's silly old hens."

"Your genes are too precious to squander," Delphi persisted.

"Then clone me."

"Clone you? Cloning is illegal!" Delphi hesitated, then to Morgan's surprise, said quietly, "But why not? It's illegal only because it's believed it would

105

lead to stagnation in the gene pool. In your case, of course, that would be a good thing." She laughed then added, "The real reason, I suspect, is some of the men are afraid that cloning could mean women wouldn't have any use for them at all."

"Have you cloned before?"

"No, not personally. But I know how it's done." Delphi whispered conspiratorially, "I've seen others do it."

"Would we be exactly alike, my clone and I?"

"Of course."

"I mean, spiritually?"

"Exactly alike, Morgan Quade. You would have the same proclivities, the same sensitivities — regretfully, the same temperament. The clone would lack only your memories and experience."

"How fast would it grow?"

"As fast as I tell it to." Delphi smiled. "I'd keep it at the blatula stage for a while. The idea of having two Morgan Quades would take some getting used to."

"How old would it be? When it's complete?"

"As old as you are now."

"How would it know?"

"The cells will tell it."

"I wouldn't want you to get into any trouble on my account, Delphi."

Delphi, however, seemed quite taken with her new adventure.

"Oh, what can they do to me?" she said carelessly. "I'm an old woman. Some think I'm already in my dotage. They'll assume I forgot to add the remainder of the genetic material. Or they'll think the sperm was genetically blank. That

106

happens. Once your cells have divided, they won't interfere. That would be murder."

"Is the procedure difficult?"

"Not at all," said Delphi briskly. "All I need do is scrape a few cells from the lining of the buccal cavity. It's ridiculously simple."

Delphi selected a synthetic blade and a bottle of generative bath. The blade was an old-fashioned dermatome, used mainly for teaching purposes. She returned to the examining table and eyed Morgan expectantly. "Open wide," she said cheerfully.

Chapter 8

The Amphitheater of the Sciences was exactly like the amphitheaters serving the other disciplines — built after the Greek fashion, stark and white and startlingly beautiful in its simplicity. The seats rose in semicircles from the depressed stage, wide steps cut out of great blocks of marble.

The amphitheaters seemed curiously out of place at the half-millennium, such solid permanence an aberration in a universe of mobile modules. The buildings were very old, having been commissioned by the world body almost seven hundred years before to provide an international center for the study of the sciences and humanities. Now, at the half-millennium, they were revered for their beauty and their spirituality. People came to them for knowledge — often of a rather specific variety — but also for spiritual refreshment. It was possible, even on a busy day with the auditorium in full session, to slip into a seat in the back row behind the supporting columns and find almost perfect solitude, so vast were the walls, so high the ceilings, so airy the atmosphere.

Antiquity was not scheduled to speak until twelve but arrived several minutes ahead of time. She liked to walk about for a time and study the high ceilings and walls before taking her place at the lectern. The ceiling particularly interested her. It was painted not in murals or elaborate designs but in the pure colors of skies long past, and sunlight. She could see an ancient sky, feel the wind fresh off a grassy field bedecked with wildflowers and crisscrossed by narrow paths and perhaps a small winding brook. She could hear stillness and imagine the rustling noises of tall trees.

Antiquity walked the perimeter of the amphitheater, her eyes trained on the ceiling, until a soft white light flickered, sending a shimmering arc of light about the auditorium. The light meant the lecture would begin in five minutes.

Her audience trickled in. Gaggles of fresh-faced school children, brought in from sub-Oceana on a day trip, sat in the middle rows. Groups came from the Academy, serious young adults studying for degrees, each carrying a recording device and several blank disks. Engineers, technologists, professors and ordinary citizens filtered in, singly or in small groups. As Antiquity glanced over the audience, she was pleased to see that Delphi was present.

So was Morgan Quade. Antiquity caught sight of her in the last row, her head resting against the wall, her feet propped insolently on the seat in front of her. Antiquity snorted. Morgan Quade listening with half an ear heard more than most people with two. She found her insouciance galling nevertheless. It had been a sore point between them in her student days.

Jaffey had arrived late and sat with Millgrew and Marcus Vinkle on the aisle to the left of the lectern. Jaffey smiled and waved but Antiquity merely nodded curtly. She regarded Marcus as flippant and disrespectful.

Antiquity regretted Deirdre's absence but realized it was unavoidable. One of the herring gulls had commenced to set on a nest of eggs. The mother was inexperienced and Deirdre had to be available in case it was necessary to rescue the eggs.

Antiquity waited until she had the attention of her audience. "You have come here, expecting to hear the latest in a series of philosophical dissertations," she began. Her voice sounded shrill and thin against the vastness of the amphitheater. "I have taken the liberty of changing my topic for this session. I hope no one will be inconvenienced."

The students and those professors who had rehearsed questions and made other preparations, groaned. The school children looked to their patrons expectantly.

"Today, I want to talk about distant energy sources, their output and the objective measure of this output," Antiquity continued stiffly. "Specifically I wish to discuss the sun." She reached into the curtains behind her and drew out a table holding an object covered with a square of cloth. Antiquity removed the cloth. "I am sure everyone recognizes the portable neutrino counter. An old but reliable instrument that has, regrettably, fallen into disuse of late." She folded the cloth and placed it on the cart beside the object. "Today, I plan to speak at length about the neutrino counter, its suitability as a measuring device and its relevance to modern applied physics."

There was a muffled explosion as Marcus Vinkle leaned forward, attempting to mask a loud guffaw in a sneeze. Jaffey sat bold upright, her lips parted in astonishment. Millgrew frowned and sniffed slightly.

"A neutrino," Antiquity said clearly, "is a particle without electrical charge or mass, traveling at the speed of light. In ancient times, the neutrino was believed to be the result of a nuclear reaction at the core of the sun. Today we know that neutrinos, in fact, emanate from the near layer, the near layer being the area of burning solar gases nearest the most peripheral insulator layer. Neutrino production should be particularly intense in this near layer. After all, it is the near layer that must reach the critical temperature necessary to ignite the gases in the insulating layer." Antiquity turned toward the children in the middle rows and said indulgently, "The formula, please."

"It = ct x m x ms/cf," chortled an eager moppet.

"Quite right, where m stands for time in milliseconds and cf represents a stable factor, estimating neutrino friction." She continued, strolling

111

toward the left of the stage, "Ancient neutrino measuring devices were crude, cumbersome devices of enormous size. Often they were secreted away in tunnels and abandoned mine shafts. They required great quantities of liquid chemicals for their operation. The most recent neutrino counter is, however, rather small, possessing a special tylenium filter to eliminate random cosmic radiation. This instrument," she said fondly, "is, admittedly, quite an antique, being well over five hundred years old. The truth of the matter is, once constructed, the portable neutrino counter proved to be so reliable, so precise, it has not been necessary to improve on its original design."

The recorders belonging to the students from the Academy began to whir wildly. The children in the middle rows craned their necks, attracted by the sudden activity of the machines.

Antiquity went on. "SOLCOM is, of course, of more recent vintage. It is worth mentioning that, originally, the instruments of SOLCOM were set according to the readings of this very neutrino counter. More recently, SOLCOM was adjusted to reflect new models of solar constants. This," said Antiquity, with a slightly disparaging sniff, "produced results slightly different than those of the neutrino counter but not significantly so. There is evidence lately, however, that some of SOLCOM's measurements may be gravely in error. Most recently —"

A dozen hands shot up. Antiquity's own hand rose to demand silence.

"For the past six months, the neutrino counter has shown an alarming decrease in the numbers of neutrinos reaching the inner cell, evidence the number of neutrinos has been significantly reduced or available neutrinos are less active or both." She paused for a moment, then added almost casually, "Whatever is the case, we may be faced with a solar power failure of major proportions."

The students looked at each other and at their professors. They knew what they were hearing was preposterous but they hadn't the courage to challenge the venerable science-philosopher. Several eyes shifted rather hopefully to the engineers who sat on the aisle. Jaffey stared straight ahead. Millgrew seemed absorbed by her cuff buttons. Marcus sat forward, his face cupped in his hands, his shoulders trembling.

Finally, one of the professors spoke. "Antiquity," she said politely, "surely the discrepancies you mention could be the result of counter error. Many of our fine technologists, while conceding the basic soundness of the counter, agree that it is subject, occasionally, to unpredictable and fairly significant errors."

Antiquity stared at the professor, her nostrils pinched with derision. "I am quite aware that the counter is subject to occasional error. I have taken full account of that fact in compiling my data. As you may know, professor, I taught the theory of solar constants at the Academy years ago. Obviously, you didn't take my class."

"Perhaps we could get the opinion of one of the engineers," said one of the bolder students.

All eyes turned immediately toward Jaffey and Marcus.

Marcus stared at the floor for a moment, then

with a sigh, stood up. "We have no evidence SOLCOM is malfunctioning. As you know," he added, nodding in the direction of the students, "the system is subject to constant verification."

There was a long, uneasy silence, then Antiquity turned to Marcus and said coolly, "Then why did you elect to proceed to teardown?"

Marcus stared at Antiquity, bewildered. "I beg your pardon?"

"Teardown," Antiquity persisted. "Isn't that the term engineers use when they overhaul a system?" She stared at Marcus.

Marcus looked to Jaffey for help but Jaffey studiously avoided his gaze. "We treat all discrepancies seriously," he said. "It would be injudicious to do otherwise."

Antiquity smiled lightly. "I see," she said. "And what portion of our resources would a teardown consume, Mr. Vinkle? Would it be five percent?"

"I would imagine that it would be closer to three," said Marcus wearily.

"Three!" Antiquity raised her eyebrows. "Isn't that a rather large expenditure for an individual project?"

"Perhaps."

"All because everyone at SOLCOM is too stubborn to trust the findings of the neutrino counter," said Antiquity easily. "Or perhaps you believe what the neutrino counter has to say. Perhaps the engineers are in a state of panic because SOLCOM is malfunctioning."

"No state of panic exists," said Marcus as evenly as possible. "We simply believe any challenge to the veracity of SOLCOM must be taken seriously. A system as important as SOLCOM demands this."

"You are willing to spend three percent of our resources," said Antiquity softly, "to repair a system that isn't broken, all because of a neutrino counter that you, yourself, have referred to as a piece of junk. Either SOLCOM is mad or your opinion of the counter has improved dramatically, Mr. Vinkle."

The smile that played constantly about the lips of Marcus Vinkle disappeared. The veins at his temple began to bulge ominously, but Marcus took a deep breath and said mildly, "The floor is yours, Antiquity."

For a moment Antiquity hesitated, disarmed by her easy victory. Then, with a slight smile, she turned away and launched into the body of her address.

When the lecture ended, Jaffey strained to catch snippets of conversations. It was soon obvious that the students hadn't taken Antiquity seriously. They found her theory shocking but flimsy and, in the end, unconvincing — for more than one reason.

Normally, Antiquity could win over any group simply with her persuasive command of the literature. Today, however, two-thirds of the way through her lecture, she had drawn a serious blank. She had stood on the stage, flushed and helpless until a student asked a question that jogged her memory.

Marcus didn't speak until he and Jaffey were outside the building. "The old fool!" he said with a savage laugh. "We've fibbed about the teardown to protect her integrity and now she turns on us and makes us look foolish!"

"She's confused," said Jaffey unhappily. "You saw how disoriented she became toward the end of the lecture. Fortunately, no one believed her. I think we can pass her claims off as an attempt to be provocative, to stimulate discussion. Antiquity has used that tactic many times before."

"Damned old fool!" Marcus's face was red with anger.

The news reports that evening said only that the lecture had been well-received. None of the reporters mentioned Antiquity's mental lapse. Nor did any of them comment upon her exchange with Marcus. The content of the speech was described as "a review of ancient energy-measuring devices." The President, after receiving Marcus's report, had contacted the editors, asking them to treat Antiquity gently. Out of loyalty and respect they agreed.

Chapter 9

"Breadcrumbs," said Morgan.

"I beg your pardon?" Jaffey said.

"The noise is caused by breadcrumbs," said Morgan mildly. "We have the same problem when Shenkel eats his lunch in the cockpit. The crumbs get into the instrument panel, into the AV recording devices. Sometimes —"

"It can't be!" Jaffey stared at Millgrew who had begun to nod slightly.

"I must confess," said Millgrew slowly, "it never crossed my mind it might be breadcrumbs. Of course,

I've never heard breadcrumbs in our systems before. Rather fine ones, I expect. I'll have to run a comparative test."

"Gerald!" said Jaffey in disgust. "If that errant technician has fouled the SOLCOM receptor with breadcrumbs, I'll see he's demoted to the cleanup crew."

"We didn't *see* any breadcrumbs," said Millgrew cautiously.

"We weren't looking for breadcrumbs," said Jaffey crossly. "We were looking for dust and lint. Breadcrumbs are sticky. They've probably lodged around the seals at the entry sites." She stood up, arching her back. "We'll have to go over the surface again with moisture-sensitive resin detectors. I'll bet Marcus will have a good chuckle about having the chief engineer cleaning breadcrumbs out of his vents. For free too. My time is coming out of *my* budget."

"Do you think the breadcrumbs could have caused a malfunction?" Morgan asked suddenly.

Jaffey shook her head. "No, they cause an unpleasant background noise. Eventually, they could make transmissions extremely fuzzy. They wouldn't create a quantitative change though."

"Perhaps a routine crew could take over now," Millgrew suggested hopefully.

Jaffey started to put her tools away. "No, we'll do it. I have to be here for the Assembly in a week anyway. I have no compelling reason to return to Zeta Base at the moment. The Academy is thrilled to have you here, Millgrew. The students are delighted to see you face to face. We may as well stay and see the job through. Besides, Antiquity wouldn't be satisfied if she thought I had palmed the job off half-finished. She won't trust anyone else's results."

Morgan fixed Jaffey with a solid stare. "Are those your only reasons?" she asked sweetly.

Jaffey smiled slightly. "They're the reasons that will go into the report."

Morgan picked up her camera bag. "Perhaps the chief engineer should conduct her private business on her own time at her own expense," she said with a smirk. "That would make a great story for an exposé journalist." She shook her head, then swung her bag to her shoulder, suddenly businesslike. "Will you start the review tomorrow?"

"Probably, provided Marcus gets the report to the President first thing and she doesn't dawdle over the approval."

"Good," she said briskly. "I'll see you tomorrow then."

"Tomorrow." Jaffey turned to Millgrew. "Let's do our report and get out of here. I'm getting a headache."

When the report was finished, Jaffey and Millgrew returned to the Grand Hotel and enjoyed a sumptuous meal to celebrate the end of the gruelling task — even if it did have to be repeated.

"I have to go to the compound," Jaffey said. "Antiquity wants me to drop by at eight. I presume she wants a preliminary report of the results of the teardown."

Millgrew paused, hoping Jaffey would invite her to go along. It was apparent the idea hadn't crossed Jaffey's mind. Millgrew said dolefully, "I think I'll stay in and try my chess set."

"Well," said Jaffey with a sigh. "I'm sure you'll

119

find Bialosky's games more fun than an evening with Antiquity. I'm afraid she's becoming difficult. Her mood changes daily. She's beside herself with anxiety. Hostile at times. People are beginning to avoid her. She talks of nothing but her strange theories. I'm worried her competence will be called into question and she will be deprived of her honors. I can't imagine what that would do to her."

"It would be a great disgrace," said Millgrew solemnly, "to be removed from office for reason of insanity."

"Yes, it would." Jaffey tossed her serviette onto the table. "Don't wait up for me, Millgrew," she said. She winked. "With any luck, I may run into Deirdre."

"Yes, of course," said Millgrew quietly.

At eight that evening, Alix Windsor's flagship came into port at the far side of Earth Station 1.

"So, this is Earth Station 1," said the young navigator to her. "It's nothing but a crude docking facility. I was expecting something more elaborate."

"It's a piece of history," said Alix, intrigued. She leaned over the navigator's shoulder to get a better view of the docks. "These stations were built years ago as emergency depots. Now they're part of Strategic Command directly under the President. They're stocked continuously with survival gear and used for elementary survival training and emergency repairs."

"You mean they're unpopulated!" the navigator cried. "No shore leave!"

"I'm afraid not." Alix turned to the first officer. "Please take command of the bridge and make sure the crew is comfortable. I'll be in my cabin."

From her port she could see Earth and her moon, pale blots against a gloomy canvas. She lay against her pillow and wondered what Earth would be like. She had seen the films of course, but real life was never quite like its representation. She watched the pale planet with fascination.

The people of Leith and Xerxes had never been able to understand her romance with Earth. They were a pragmatic people, always looking to the future, always looking outward. Earth was the dying planet. Isn't that what they said in the Middle and New Colonies? Oh, she might go on for half an eternity but her best years — the lush, vibrant years of growth and fresh perspectives were behind her. Alix had heard these assessments and opinions as a child. But rather than deter her, they had fueled her imagination and, indeed, her love.

Finally, reluctantly, Alix darkened the porthole. It had been a long flight and she needed to rest. Within hours, the President would call and she would feel the soil of her ancestral lands.

By the time Millgrew reached her room, she realized she had left her chess set at SOLCOM. One of the technicians had challenged her to a match over the lunch hour and she had carelessly forgotten the game in the staff lounge. She left the hotel and hopped the first mass transit vehicle to SOLCOM.

Two hours after Alix Windsor docked at Earth Station 1, Anatole Zog brought the Second Fleet to rest at adjacent anchor. Then, having carried out the obligatory status reports to the Territorial Fleet, he retired to his capsule and treated himself to steam inhalation.

One hour later, the First Fleet leapt from hyperspace, geared to Cruz 3 and glided to take up command position at Earth Station 1. Oliva Stern contacted Commander Windsor, inviting her to take drinks with her in her cabin.

The three fleets of the Union swung silently at anchor, poised within a stone's throw of Earth.

SOLCOM at night was as dark and silent as a tomb. The administrative offices were secured, as were the auxiliary stations where SOLCOM's functions had been rerouted for the duration of the teardown.

Millgrew was surprised to see a light on in the solar receptor chamber. She slid toward the door, glancing about curiously. Two technicians sat before the monitors, chatting and laughing between themselves. Millgrew coughed discreetly.

The technicians spun about startled, then, seeing

Millgrew, relaxed. "We don't often get visitors at night," said the younger technician.

"I'm very sorry," Millgrew murmured. "I came to get my chess set."

"I'll take a look." The younger technician obligingly vaulted out of her chair and disappeared toward the staff lounge.

"We're off auxiliary," the older technician explained. "The orders to reactivate the system came down a couple of hours ago. We've just completed the switch. I guess everything was OK. The system was given a clean bill of health."

"Indeed," Millgrew murmured.

The older technician was silent, his eyes fixed on the screen in front of him. Millgrew stood very still, a hand cupped behind one ear.

"The static's most annoying," Millgrew said. "It must be difficult to tolerate."

"It started a couple of months ago. You'd hardly notice it at all after a while."

"Breadcrumbs," Millgrew whispered. "Yes, that has to be the answer."

The younger technician returned to the room. She held the chess set out eagerly.

"What were you saying about breadcrumbs?" asked the older technician.

Millgrew tucked the chess set safely within her cloak. "Oh, it was nothing, nothing at all," she said apologetically. "Theoretical gibberish."

"Who knows what goes on," said the older technician. He stared into the monitor, then sighed. "Sometimes," he said, "I could swear I'm watching the same thing, over and over again."

* * * * *

The compound was a dimly lit collection of boxlike modules, bound together by a windbreak of unpretentious cinder blocks. Jaffey walked through the gate and crossed the courtyard to Antiquity's loft, climbed the outside steps and vaulted onto the balcony. She tapped gently against the glass of the French windows. She couldn't see even the faintest shard of light. She pushed against the window, straining to see through the thin curtain.

Antiquity had apparently stepped out of the apartment for a moment or had fallen asleep. Jaffey ran down the steps and crossed the compound to the sanctuary. It too was in darkness. A lone worker lingered near the door to the sheep pen.

"Have you seen Antiquity?" Jaffey asked. "She asked me to meet her at her apartment at eight."

The worker shrugged. "She left several minutes ago," he said. "I think it's her night to play cards with old Nadril."

Jaffey shook her head, exasperated. Antiquity had forgotten all about her. A frame of light on the opposite side of the square caught her eye. The light came from Deirdre's third floor loft. Jaffey could not believe her good fortune. She ran across the courtyard, leapt exuberantly to the third step and ran up the staircase, taking the steps two at a time.

Deirdre opened the door at the first knock. She was wearing a pure white soft-weave robe pulled tight at the neck. "Jaffey," she said, startled. "Why, I —"

Jaffey looked at her, beaming. "Is it all right if I

come in or do I have to talk to you while swinging from the railing like one of your apes?"

"Yes — of course — come in." Deirdre turned quickly from the door.

"I came out to see Antiquity," said Jaffey. "Unfortunately, she's forgotten about me and has gone out for the evening."

"She's so careless about her appointments," Deirdre said ruefully. "No matter how I try to organize her —"

Jaffey surveyed her, a slight smile on her lips, her eyes searching. "You've been avoiding me," she said.

Deirdre shook her head. "No, not at all," she said stiffly. "I've been very busy. I've had students."

Jaffey's smile widened. "I'm glad to see it's not just teasing about your animals that arouses your passion."

"No," she said caustically. "It's also those who come to my home unannounced and waste my time with unfounded, adolescent accusations."

"No, you have been avoiding me, Deirdre. You've been avoiding me because you're reluctant to face the truth."

"The truth? And what would that be?"

"That you're in love with me," said Jaffey easily. "That you've always been in love with me."

"You had your chance," said Deirdre in a low voice. "You were unfaithful."

Jaffey turned to her, her gaze cool and appraising. "You've been with Morgan," she said. "You don't seem to have any problem tolerating her infidelities."

125

Deirdre flushed. "It's not the same thing," she said shakily. "With Morgan it's art. She draws from — for her work —"

"Then we are all artists," Jaffey said quietly. She circled the room, then stopped in front of Deirdre. "You put on this facade," she whispered, "a cool, porcelain mask. Delicate. Untouchable. Devoted daughter. Willing slave. Between us there's none of that. Only the passion between equals. I know you. I know what you're capable of. The heights you can reach . . ."

There was a long silence. Then Deirdre's arms encircled Jaffey's neck, her lips crushing hers, warm and insistent. Jaffey's head spun from the sudden turn of events as Deirdre's fingers tore at the tunic buttons.

The tunic fell to the floor with a soft thud. Deirdre's hands explored the downy undershirt, smoothing it at the shoulders, fingering the tiny fasteners.

Jaffey took a deep breath as Deirdre's hands fluttered over her breasts. She reached and with trembling fingers undid the ties of the robe.

Jaffey took Deirdre's hand and pulled her toward her, eyes searching hungrily — pale, perfect body, nipples pink and rigid against soft, unblemished skin.

Jaffey knelt, the warmth of her lips burning Deirdre's thighs. Deirdre sank back against the wall, clutching Jaffey's stiff, tousled hair as Jaffey's tongue moved deep into her.

* * * * *

They lay on the cool marble floor, wet and gently swollen, nuzzling each other gently. They were silent for a long time.

Finally Jaffey raised herself on one elbow and leaned over Deirdre, smiling. "Remember the darkness?" she whispered. "We made love until it was so dark we could scarcely see one another. We were almost carried away on the surf. We were so aroused even the cold water washing over us seemed erotic."

"I remember."

Jaffey searched Deirdre's face. "Are you ready again?" she asked.

They were interrupted by a bell — sharp, shrill, insistent. Deirdre sat bolt upright, pushing Jaffey away. "It's Morgan," she said desperately. "She's at the gate with her vehicle. She must have forgotten her pass key. She's waiting for me to let her in."

"Then don't let her in."

"She'll get in anyway. The bell will ring in the sanctuary too. One of the workers will let her in."

"Well, when she gets here, tell her to go away. Tell her you're with someone."

"I can't tell her that. She'd be devastated."

"She'll find out eventually."

"No, she can't know." Deirdre's eyes filled with tears. "She needs me, Jaffey," she whispered. "It would break her heart to find you here."

"Come," Jaffey scoffed. "I can't imagine Morgan Quade's heart would be so easily broken."

"She needs me," Deirdre repeated. She scrambled up, clutching at her robe. She gathered up Jaffey's clothing and thrust it toward her.

Jaffey lay, leaning on one elbow, watching Deirdre with evident amusement.

"Please. Go!" Deirdre turned and ran into the bathroom.

There was a muffled gush of water from behind the partially closed door. Jaffey stood and dressed reluctantly.

Deirdre appeared in the doorway, drops of water clinging to her cheeks. "Jaffey, you have to understand."

Jaffey pulled Deirdre toward her, looking deep into her eyes. "When will I see you again?"

"I don't know." Deirdre stared over Jaffey's shoulder. "Jaffey, you'll have to leave by the staircase."

Jaffey struggled into her boots. "I hope she takes the stairs this time," she said ruefully. "I think it would be best if we confronted one another."

With a good-natured laugh Jaffey kissed Deirdre's hand, then slipped through the door to the balcony.

Deirdre was in the shower when Morgan entered the apartment. Approaching the bed where Morgan lay, Deirdre came to her, sliding into her embrace, burying her face in her hair.

"You smell wonderful," Morgan said drowsily. "I'm ashamed to confess I may fall asleep on you."

"It's all right," Deirdre said quickly. She raised her head for a moment, then fell back against Morgan's shoulder. "I wasn't anticipating —"

Morgan laughed softly. "I know what you mean." She took a deep breath. "I'm absolutely exhausted but I've had the most wonderful day, Deirdre. Alf swiped my flight clearance but I was able to get on a hydrofoil at the Institute. The pilot was Lynn

MacPherson. She was exploring a new underwater eruption off Astralasia. I got some astonishing photographs. We used lungs. It was wonderful to use lungs again. It's been ages since I did any free diving." She smiled, pressing her lips against Deirdre's hair. "Maybe Alf's right. I do need a rest. That little excursion tired me more than it should have."

Morgan sighed, inhaling the fragrance of Deirdre's hair. "Your hair smells of apple blossoms, lilacs, all sorts of delicate, fresh things." She smiled. "Who knows? I may revive."

"Would you like some tea?" Deirdre pulled herself away and stood up. "It will take just a minute."

Morgan was tired to the point of restlessness. Objects, rays of light imposed themselves upon her with startling clarity but without pattern — like the shiny object on the floor, the object that bounced light into her eyes when she tilted her head at a certain angle. She reached out with one hand, wriggling down in the bed, straining as the object evaded her outstretched fingertips.

Finally, she captured the object. It was a simple obsidian disk on Andalusian silver — an engineering divisional badge. She turned the disk over in her palm.

Jaffey, C.E.

Morgan stared at the badge for a moment, annoyed and puzzled. When had Jaffey been in Deirdre's apartment? Had she dropped the badge in the courtyard the evening she dined with Antiquity? Morgan shook her head. No, that wasn't possible. She had seen the badge on Jaffey's tunic that very morning at SOLCOM. Morgan turned the badge in her hand. The clasp was broken. Tufts of fabric clung to the ragged edges. Caught on something. Ripped. Perhaps —

Ripped from a red tunic in a state of passion. Morgan stared hard at the object. The badge. The late shower. Deirdre's nervousness. "Damn you, Jaffey," she whispered.

"Morgan, would you like a little honey in your tea?" Deirdre's voice floated from the kitchen.

"Yes," she managed to say.

She continued to stare at the badge, her mind numb. She thrust the badge quickly into the breast pocket of her fatigues as Deirdre appeared in the doorway. Was it her imagination or did Deirdre look guilty?

Deirdre put the tea on the table and sat down on the bed. "I don't think you're going to revive," she said gently. "You look even more tired than before."

Morgan smiled and looked away. "You're so good to me," she said, sipping her tea.

Deirdre went into the bathroom while Morgan undressed, returning with a basin of water and a soft cloth. She sat on the bed beside her and carefully washed her hands and face.

"Is there anything else I can do?" she said at last.

Morgan's eyes were closed. "No," she whispered, "just come to bed."

Jaffey arrived at the hotel, breathless. Millgrew was waiting up for her with a message.

"What's happened to you?" Millgrew blurted. "You look as though you've been attacked."

"I assure you it was a most pleasant attack," said Jaffey, laughing. She plopped down on the bed, tearing at the envelope Millgrew handed her.

The message was written on the official stationary of the Union, initialed by the President herself. Jaffey read it aloud.

Jaffey,
Sorry. Can't permit teardown at this time. President's orders. Do me a favor though. The President would like an evaluation of the energy requirements for the greenhouse effect at -40. With all the givens, please.

It was signed Marcus Vinkle. Millgrew looked at Jaffey, worried, but Jaffey laughed and stuffed the message into her pocket.

"Marcus Vinkle is either very obtuse or very smug," she told Millgrew. "It seems he's managed to hoodwink the President into palming his tedious tasks off onto us. I've a good mind to take him to task for it."

"Quite," said Millgrew stiffly. "I was at SOLCOM tonight to pick up my chess set. The system had already been transferred from auxiliary."

"Really?" Jaffey shrugged her lack of interest. "Well, it's the President's decision."

"And the other?"

Jaffey reviewed the message with a grimace. "We'll do it, of course," she said. "But only because we can accomplish the task a hundred times faster than the SOLCOM technicians. It's perfectly mindless work." She sighed and flopped back on the bed. "Perhaps perfect for someone with my present mind-set." She propped herself up on her elbows, the grimace turning into a rueful smile. "Look at me. I didn't have time to fasten my cuff buttons. Badge ripped off — If I were a cadet or a junior officer I'd be drummed out of the corps for appearing this way in public." She laughed. "Have you ever had to scramble to avoid the wrath of an angry partner?"

"No." Millgrew turned away, embarrassed. "No, I've never had to do anything of that sort."

"She's in love with me," Jaffey murmured. "Deirdre's in love with me, Millgrew. I knew it would happen."

"I thought she was very close to Morgan Quade," said Millgrew weakly. Her cheeks were flushed.

"She loves us both," she mused. "She always has. But she's in love with me. It was easy for her while I was away. She didn't have to choose. She always found that painful. Now I'm here. She has to make a decision. She knows neither of us will share her with the other."

"No, of course not. That wouldn't be right." Millgrew began to edge toward the bathroom door.

"She's in love with me," Jaffey repeated. "She claims to be bound to Morgan. She says Morgan needs her. Funny, I've never known Morgan to need anyone."

"I wouldn't know," said Millgrew quickly.

"Surely she's bound mainly by guilt," Jaffey murmured. "I wouldn't think — Millgrew!" She glanced up as Millgrew disappeared into the bathroom. "Damn," she said. She picked up the dream recorder and looked at it for a moment. Then, with a smile, she tossed it into the drawer.

Chapter 10

When Morgan Quade arrived at SOLCOM the next morning, she was directed immediately to Marcus Vinkle. Marcus informed her, pleasantly, that the teardown was complete and Jaffey and Millgrew had been assigned to other tasks.

"These things happen," he said with a nervous giggle. "Yesterday's compelling issue is today's dead horse." All the time he spoke, he played with a pair of disks that lay on the desk in front of him. Finally, with a sweep of his large hand, he edged them into the drawer. "I don't know why you seem so surprised, Morgan," he said lightly. "I informed your desk first thing this morning."

"I haven't been to the office and I haven't picked up my messages."

"Well, Alf can fill you in."

"I see." Morgan glanced about the room, apparently unperturbed. "Do you happen to have a press kit?" she asked with a sudden smile. "I neglected to ask Jaffey and Millgrew some of the most basic questions. Now," she said with a shrug, "they're gone and I have a deadline."

"No problem, no problem," he fluttered. "Stay right where you are. I'll get you a kit from the library."

Morgan looked about quickly, then went immediately to the desk drawer and removed the disks. She replaced them with two new blanks from her jacket pocket. When Marcus returned, she was sitting in the chair flipping through a copy of *The History of SOLCOM.* He handed her a small box containing several stacks of promotional disks.

She reviewed the disks at her console. The press kit was the usual upbeat production of dry, scientific data and departmental hype. The disks she had filched from the desk drawer were totally incomprehensible. Obviously the documents were classified. It would take a full review of a committee of council to change the classification. Sometimes the process took weeks.

She took the press kit to Alf and dropped it onto his desk. She placed the pilfered disks in a packet and put it into her pocket.

"Well, we can't do much with the story anyway," Alf said when she told him what happened.

"Obviously, the whole thing was a sham, a sop to Antiquity."

She told him she was taking the remainder of the day off.

When she left the news building, she had the distinct impression she was being watched. She walked along very slowly, glancing about nonchalantly for signs of surveillance. Out of the corner of her eye, she caught brief flashes — silent ghosts of rapid evasive movement — which disappeared when she turned her head. Someone or something was following her.

Her destination was the public library. She chose a deliberately circuitous route. She reached the steps leading up to the main entrance and paused, glancing at her chronometer. Then, as if suddenly remembering her purpose, she turned and ran quickly up the steps.

The library was a labyrinth of white floors and ceilings and gray computer banks with thousands of terminals. The upper floors housed the archives — several rooms of ancient, dusty volumes sealed permanently in environment-controlled chambers. The research materials were stored in the stacks — subterranean mazes packed to capacity with millions of audio-visual disks.

Morgan ran down the steps to the third stack level and dropped behind a pillar. Within seconds a shadow flickered across the stairwell. She ran down two more flights. Once again the shadow appeared and disappeared. She ducked into the washroom, took the disks from the packet and inspected them thoroughly. There were no telltale signs to indicate the disks had been marked. Marcus, she guessed, had discovered the switch and had had her followed on speculation. She left the washroom and looked about quickly. A shadow moved across the doorway at the far end of the stack. She ducked behind a shelf and scribbled a note. She put the note into the packet with the disks and coded it to Jaffey at the Grand Hotel. She then ran to the bottom stack, dropping the packet into the pneumatic tube system used to deliver materials to government offices and visiting officials housed in the area hotels.

Morgan left the library by the rear door and ran for several blocks, weaving and backtracking periodically, hoping to reach the news building undetected. Her personal vehicle was parked in the lot at the back. She jumped into it and drove to the compound.

The sky was cloudy and a fine haze hung over the water. Deirdre was tending her flock. Morgan crept forward silently, concealing herself, lying on her belly in the long grass. Deirdre waded in the cool water among the purple ocean sage, her overalls rolled to the knees. The mothers in the nests clucked to her and Deirdre spoke to them, it seemed, in their own language — they responded, crowding closer to her, nuzzling against her. Even from a distance, Morgan could see the bright, intelligent eyes flash and hear the murmured coos as they dropped closer to Deirdre's ear.

They spoke to Deirdre in ways she, Morgan, could never understand — as Deirdre would never understand the fire. Morgan watched for a time and listened, then, feeling like a voyeur, crept away.

She drove away, moving slowly and aimlessly into the great marsh. The grass was sparse at this time

137

of year, brittle and brown, musty like old cornhusks and garden mulch. Morgan drove until the marsh grass gave way to the soft sand and rolling dunes. There, within sight of the water, she got out of the vehicle.

Out there the world was an understatement — dull gray skies, moody gray-green water, faded earth tones. People didn't come here. It was death. It was the end of the world, that place children dream of when they are too young to understand the truths of science. Adults said it was more depressing than the empty coldness of remote space. It was in them; it was a part of them.

"Your eyes, Morgan, your eyes," Delphi had said, her own eyes full of trouble. "The damage is subtle but unmistakable. In one month, two at the best, the fine sensitivity to color will be gone."

"You can give me a transplant, Delphi. Transplants are easy."

"It wouldn't be the same," said Delphi, her voice barely a whisper. "You are an artist, Morgan Quade. Your eyes are unique."

Morgan stared out over the water, Delphi's words echoing in the whispers of the marsh grass. *We have lost you, Morgan Quade. We have lost you to the fires.*

She walked to the water's edge, staring out over the ocean, squinting to catch sight of a huge wave in the distance. To be a blind artist or an impostor, seeing the world through mindless eyes — the prospect was bleak. Should she conserve her sight, play it safe with what remained or should she take a chance, go after the big one, that glorious adventure that might reward her with something more dazzling than she had ever imagined? And what of Deirdre? Should she continue to fight for her, knowing what she now knew?

A flash appeared on the water to her left, a tiny flash of light, quickly fluttered by the rippling waters. She took a deep breath and held it. Suddenly they loomed behind her. Four of them. She turned, driving a straight-arm into the midsection of the first. The second lunged for her but she turned him aside with a chop to the shoulder. She turned and sprinted toward her vehicle. They were shouting to her. She paid no attention. The shots came with startling brutality. The first hit her in the shoulder. She fell to one knee then wrenched herself upright, pulling at the dart. It came free, covered with blood and tiny pieces of flesh. The second shot hit her in the upper arm. She staggered, pulling at it with her good hand. Then they struck, three quick hard shots to the neck. The breath exploded out of her body and she collapsed against the side of her vehicle. The blood poured down her arm and soaked the back of her hair and tunic.

The pounding feet came to an abrupt halt. The pursuers approached quietly.

"Is she dead?" asked one.

"I don't know," said another.

Jaffey and Millgrew had spent most of the day at the Academy library, returning to the hotel at about 1500 hours.

"I think I've received a gift," she told Millgrew, taking a packet from her message unit. "It's from

Morgan Quade," she said, surprised. She showed the note to Millgrew.

Millgrew frowned. "I'm afraid I don't recognize the language," she confessed.

"I'm not sure if I do either," said Jaffey with a smile. "At least not anymore. It's a secret code we invented in kindergarten." Finally she turned to Millgrew and said, "I think I've got it."

Jaffey,
These are from Marcus Vinkle's desk drawer.
I think he's up to something. Can you read?

Jaffey inserted the first disk into her console. "Hm, top secret," she murmured.

Millgrew paled at the mention of "top secret" and retreated across the room.

Jaffey shook her head. "It's a tape of solar activity, dated yesterday. A routine recording. I have no idea why it was classified. Someone must have a taste for intrigue." Jaffey viewed the tape for several more minutes, then removed the disk, inserted the second disk. "It's a solar recording too," she said presently. "Also dated yesterday." She glanced at the chronometer in the corner of the film. "This is odd. The recordings appear to have been taken at the same time. I wonder if they routinely take multiple tapes. It would seem to be a waste of time."

Millgrew coughed dryly. "Teaching purposes, perhaps."

"They don't look quite alike," said Jaffey thoughtfully.

Millgrew was edging closer to the console as Jaffey spoke. "Perhaps the recordings reflect different angles."

"No, the coordinates are identical. The recordings are standard views." Jaffey said, "Put the other disk in your console, Millgrew. Let's have a look at them, side-by-side."

"Same time, same day," said Jaffey after a few minutes, "but the recordings are quite different. Very different. It doesn't make sense."

"We need an interpreter," said Millgrew.

"Hm," Jaffey squinted into the screen. "It's been years since I've tried to read a solar tracing but the red one is thermal and the blue one —" She paused, then said with a grimace, "Well, it doesn't matter. They're obviously different. All of the values in the second are significantly lower than the first."

"The neutrino values are eight and six-point-nine, Millgrew said. "It's a new calculation I've been working on. By comparing the amplitude of the waves we can indirectly —"

"But six-point-nine is not acceptable," Jaffey said, perplexed. "That really suggests — do we have audio?"

Simultaneously, they pushed the volume equation. A hush fell over the room, the only sound the whir of the disks.

Suddenly, Jaffey pointed to Millgrew's console.

Together they said, "Breadcrumbs!"

Jaffey stared at Millgrew, open-mouthed. "Someone's hot-wired the system."

* * * * *

Jaffey arrived at SOLCOM at 1600 hours. Leaving her vehicle unsecured in the parking lot, she ran toward the main gate.

The door refused to budge. Jaffey tried her key once more, then began to pound vigorously. Presently a guard appeared. Jaffey showed her security clearance. The guard looked at it without interest, then said politely. "All passes are temporarily frozen. There's been a theft."

"I have to see Marcus Vinkle at once." Jaffey touched the guard lightly on the chest, then rushed past him. The guard glanced about uncertainly, then followed at a dog trot.

The corridors of SOLCOM were gloomy and deserted. Jaffey ran, the soft rubber soles of her boots whooshing against the dense marble tiles, the technicians in the receptor room looking up in surprise as she dashed past.

A guard appeared at the opposite end of the corridor. He pointed a stun gun rather uncertainly in Jaffey's direction. Jaffey pushed Marcus Vinkle's door open quickly and stepped inside.

Marcus Vinkle sat hunched over a console at the far end of the room, flanked on the right by SOLCOM's chief solar technologist and on the left by the President's solar advisor. Jaffey stepped forward, her eyes riveted to the screen.

Marcus Vinkle spun about in his chair. "Jaffey!" His face broke into a large, nervous grin. "What are you doing here?"

The guard bolted through the door, gun poised, looking to Marcus for guidance. Marcus held up a hand.

"Something very strange is going on here," said

Jaffey, breathless. She took the disks from her pocket. "I think these require an explanation."

Marcus stood up, his eyes fixed on the package in Jaffey's hand. "Of course you deserve an explanation, Jaffey," he said soothingly. "But first, the disks. They were stolen, you know. That's a problem. Who knows whose hands they fell into."

Jaffey started to say no one had seen the disks but her and Millgrew, but the expression in Marcus's eyes sounded a warning. "No problem exists," she said quickly. "No one has seen the disks but me."

"Then you took them from my desk drawer," Marcus pressed.

Jaffey drew herself to her full height. "I took them for my personal use. As Chief Engineer that's well within my prerogatives."

Marcus walked toward Jaffey, his hand extended. The science advisor sat poised on the edge of his chair, scarcely breathing. The solar theorist had never taken his eyes off the console, going about his business as if intruders with stun guns were a feature of his everyday life. Marcus stopped in front of Jaffey.

"Let's have the disks, Jaffey," he said pleasantly. "I'll see they're returned to the vault."

Jaffey's fingers closed more tightly about the disks. "No," she said clearly. "If you don't mind, as Chief Engineer I'd like to hold onto these tapes a little longer."

"Perhaps you'd care to file a report with the President," said Marcus politely. "Or share them with Antiquity. I'm sure she would be interested."

Jaffey tucked the disks into her pocket and took a step backward. She hesitated as her shoulder brushed against the stun gun. "Perhaps," she suggested, smiling, "you could call off the guard, Marcus."

"Of course, Jaffey." Marcus jerked his head and the guard stepped aside.

"Good night," said Jaffey, still smiling.

"Good night, old friend," said Marcus affectionately.

Jaffey stepped outside the door and ran to the side exit. It was locked. She turned and began to walk slowly down the corridor.

Marcus turned to the guard. "That woman is escaping with stolen property," he said brightly. "Apprehend her."

Jaffey heard the door open and heard the soft footfall of the guard. She had heard the pain from a stun gun wound was unbearable. She had never been seriously injured in her life. She hoped she would be able to endure the pain and behave in a dignified manner.

"Stop, please." The guard's words echoed off the walls, shrill and hollow.

Jaffey gritted her teeth and walked on.

The stun gun discharged its pellet with a sickening thud, striking Jaffey in the neck. The breath left her body and she collapsed in a heap on the floor. She heard footsteps and saw two pairs of very large feet approaching. They seemed to move in slow motion. She struggled to get up but the deep, searing pain in the back of her neck made her moan and fall back to the floor. She lay there for what seemed an eternity, clutching her head in her hands. Finally, she passed out.

* * * * *

Jaffey opened her eyes. She was lying on a couch in the President's office. Raising one hand to shield her eyes against the glaring central light, she lay there for a few minutes while the room dipped and swerved. When the room stabilized, she was able to swing her legs over the side of the couch and sit up.

The large room was sparsely furnished. In addition to the couch and the President's desk, there were a few uncomfortable-looking chairs and little else. The walls, however, were a mosaic of information-retrieval buttons, evidence the President had the cumulative knowledge of the universe at her fingertips. The only personal touches were a painting by Morgan Quade and a potted plant Jaffey guessed was a gift from Delphi Norbert.

On an indicator panel above the door, three lights blinked softly. Jaffey stared at the panel, trying to determine its meaning. Finally, it occurred to her she was being monitored. She shrugged helplessly. The lights stopped blinking, then with one final wink, extinguished.

The President entered, with Marcus Vinkle in tow. Jaffey stood up, clutching at the wall to maintain her balance.

"I'm terribly sorry, Jaffey," said the President. "For reasons that will be clear to you shortly, it was necessary to confine you for a time. Everyone involved regrets putting you through this ordeal. Marcus regrets it. Certainly I regret it."

Jaffey shook her head and pointed to the panel above the door, groping for the appropriate words.

"The medical officer wished to monitor you until you regained consciousness," the President explained. "It's a precaution only. The initial investigation revealed no serious problem."

"I take it, then, I'm all right," said Jaffey with a feeble smile.

The President clapped her on the shoulder. "You are one hundred percent, Jaffey, as fit as a fiddle — as my learned physician mother would say." She motioned to Jaffey to sit down. "You must have many questions." The President stood in front of Jaffey. "I will give you the answers."

The President spoke for fifteen minutes. By the time she had finished, Jaffey sat, head bowed, staring at the floor, numb with shock.

"We had no choice," said Marcus defensively. "The old woman is hopelessly crazy. She'd kill us all if she had her way."

"Why did you wait so long?"

"What could we do?" asked the President. "It took forever to get data on the probabilities. We had to check and crosscheck mounds of data. We had to make sure we had the logistics to deal with an emergency."

"But why didn't you take Antiquity into your confidence?"

Marcus rolled his eyes. "As I've told you, Jaffey," he said aggressively, "the old woman is crazy. She wouldn't have cooperated. She would have been out in the streets, creating mass panic, trying to drum up support for her hare-brained schemes."

"We need your cooperation, Jaffey," the President said softly.

146

* * * * *

In the darkness of Earth Station 1, the Union Fleet stood at full alert.

Chapter 11

It was in her role of Union Counselor Exemplar that Antiquity came to the Hall, elbowing her way with unnecessary curtness through the polite throng of citizens who flocked about the main entrance. Once inside the building, she slipped into a meditation room and sank down onto one of the long wooden benches arranged in two banks, separated by a central aisle. The walls and ceiling were pure white and unadorned, the carpet dark blue and unremarkable. The benches looked very old as indeed they were, having been removed from ancient places of worship that no longer existed in any form other than piles of rubble. The benches had been restored by an art historian and for the past three centuries had graced the meditation room. The bench which Antiquity chose was marked discreetly with a small green dot, identifying its place of origin as Sub-Oceana. Antiquity knew, although not one in one hundred thousand others would that it had been taken from the abbey at Westminster.

In front of each bench was a railing, carefully fashioned to resemble the age and grain of wood in the bench, and embedded in each railing was a series of selector buttons. Pushing one of these buttons produced a holographic landscape. Normally, Antiquity selected the forest, allowing herself to be whisked away to a glen of soft whispers and delicate earth odors. Today, she selected the ocean. She wanted to think, and she hoped the roar of the waves would cut out other distractions and help her concentrate. The forest always stole her senses to the exclusion of all else.

The waves, unfortunately, had a sedative effect and within minutes she was sound asleep. She was awakened at last by a young page from the Hall who happened to stop by her bench.

"I'm sorry, Counselor," said the youngster in response to Antiquity's embarrassed spluttering. "The President's speech is about to begin. I presumed you wished to be awakened."

Antiquity merely grunted and got to her feet. For a brief but terrifying moment, she had forgotten where she was, but then she couldn't remember why she was there. She had no idea of the time of day or the date. When she reached the door of the Great

Hall, her mind had cleared but she was left feeling vulnerable and shaken.

The President arrived in the Hall at eleven o'clock precisely. She wore a simple black robe and about her neck the single, unadorned chain of office composed of metallic links, each link representing a particular planet or station. She wore it, as a rule, only during council sessions and important speeches where she wished to emphasize the diplomatic rather than the political nature of her role.

The floor of the Great Hall was sparsely occupied. Jaffey was present as were a few of the younger delegates who had come from the outer provinces, eager to see and be seen and to shake the dust of the territories from their boots. A small group of reporters sat at the back of the Hall in an area set aside for the press. Antiquity occupied the position of privilege, a separate box directly in front of the dias.

The galleries, however, were jammed with spectators. Academicians, minor bureaucrats, and citizens lucky enough to find a space filled the balconies on either side of the Hall, Millgrew among them.

The President commenced her address in the usual manner.

"My friends," she said. And when she had their attention, she added, "There is no need to panic." Throughout the gallery, spectators turned to their neighbors, puzzled. The President continued, "Two months ago, the scientists at SOLCOM detected the first signs of failure in the flow of energy from the sun."

The gallery uttered a collective gasp. All eyes

turned toward Antiquity. The old woman made a sudden choking noise, then leaned forward, her mouth working convulsively.

The President seemed oblivious to the interruption. "Marcus Vinkle, command engineer at SOLCOM, presented the facts to me immediately. Because of the grave implications of the discovery, I decided to treat the matter as high priority and confidential. Only our security advisor and key solar advisors were briefed. They were, of course, sworn to secrecy. The input from the solar receptor was directed immediately to a private monitor in the office of the command engineer. The receptor was then programmed to receive and transmit prerecorded materials from the archives. At the same time, the greenhouse effect was enhanced to maintain Earth temperatures within the normal range. Since the first warning signals, the neutrino levels have continued to decline."

The President paused to glance at her notes. "In view of this information, Marcus, my security advisor and I reviewed the records for the past several decades. In the last decade, the planet has had to import food in every year. In the decade before that the planet exported people. Together, these data suggest the planet has not been self-sufficient for at least twenty years. We are in an energy drain situation and this drain is certain to become more severe. The increased demands on our energy resources merely to maintain the greenhouse effect will be astronomical. Our scientists predict that, within months — days, if efforts to maintain the greenhouse effect are abandoned — the planet will begin to experience a severe cooling effect. The

151

cooling effect may not proceed as a steady progression but may bolt ahead in a disastrous exponential fashion. We are certain we can maintain a safe position for another three weeks. Beyond that time, we will have to make a huge energy commitment just to maintain the status quo. We predict that commitment to be in the rage of fifty percent of our total energy resources and that — if the energy drain continues in an orderly fashion, as it has over the past two months — will maintain the planet for just one Earth year. The sun's energy will run out. When it does, the earth will be frozen solid, the oceans will freeze, even the molecules of air we breathe."

There was not a sound in the room, not a whisper, not a gasp, not even a sob. The people in the galleries sat as one person, mouths agape, eyes fixed on the lectern.

The President continued to read her message, her voice strengthening with resolve. "We have considered every option. We have called forth the knowledge of our greatest solar experts. It would appear our choices of action are reduced to two. Either we evacuate the planet immediately — definitely within the next fourteen days — or we attempt to penetrate the sun with a dense nuclear probe. My advisors inform me, attractive as this second option might be, the risks are enormous. The outcome of the nuclear explosion is difficult to predict with any precision. We could create a solar inferno with a general conflagration that could incinerate not only the planets in this solar system, but several of the stations in the nearest rings. Or we could achieve a temporary respite, or we could

152

achieve absolutely nothing. The chances of an ideal outcome are judged to be no better than fifty percent. Who could accept such odds in the face of such incredible risk?"

The President paused. "There is no resource in the universe as valuable as life. Our people are too precious; we have invested too much. It is my opinion, having heard the words of my advisors and having considered them fully, Planet Earth must be mothballed."

She continued quickly, "There is no need for panic. We have assembled enough vessels to evacuate the planet within the safe period. The evacuation will include our creatures and as many native species and artifacts as is feasible. Our contingency plan — the same plan we have reviewed so thoughtfully in the past — calls for the evacuation of Earth to the New Colonies, each group to be located according to geographic origin. After the immediate phase of relocation is past, you may apply — individually or in groups — to emigrate to the colony of your choice. We have already commissioned a feasibility study with the purpose of turning the most westerly of the New Colonies into a home planet. The land is undeveloped, but the resources are there and who," she said with a faint smile, "can better lay claim to the title pioneer than the inhabitants of this planet?"

The President spoke firmly now, her words sketching the history of the species. She might as well have recited nursery rhymes. The assembly seemed frozen in time, suffocated by the enormity, like small figures on an ocean before a great storm.

"We will take no questions at this time," she said

after she had made her concluding remarks. "At noon, on the fourth day from today, a vote will be taken in the Union Council. In the meantime, we have established several in-house stations you can contact to ask questions or register complaints. These stations will be available to you on your regular console addresses." The President turned abruptly from the lectern and left.

"You!"

The voice tore the air like the rip of tartan cloth. Antiquity stood at her bench, the word frozen on her lips, her eyes hard and blue with anger. She waited then with all eyes turned to her, turned and left the Hall, her robe cutting the air behind her.

The contents of the President's address, together with her orders, were beamed to the Fleet minutes before the announcement. Oliva Stern, tears in her eyes, briefed the crew. Alix Windsor wept. Even Anatole Zog, allergic as he was, had a lump in his throat.

The President's orders were simple. The Fleet was to leave Earth Station 1 and rendezvous with Earth at ten o'clock the next morning. Purpose: Evacuate and abandon the third planet.

Chapter 12

In the days following the President's address, the planet operated in a state of controlled panic. The numbness that accompanies grief had not yet set in. It was too early to mourn and minds were still distracted with the mundane aspects of life. How would the children go to school? Would there be jobs? What possessions could be taken to the new planet?

The President went incommunicado, hearing only the voices her advisors chose to filter through. All other callers were referred to their provincial authorities.

The President had choices of her own to make. Where would she locate the new seat of government, for example? The choice was hers, as stated clearly in the Articles. She thought naturally of Asgard, her home planet, but Asgard was essentially a farming community, bereft of the sophistication necessary to be the seat of government. Perversely, she considered Omega, thinking of the disgust such a selection would create among the delegates.

Finally, after a great deal of equivocation, she chose Zeta Base, which was beautiful and cosmopolitan and much admired for its cleanliness and convenience. There would be no need to defend her choice. She selected quarters for herself and arranged to have her closest friends located nearby.

Deirdre was at wit's end with the evacuation of the sanctuary. The animals had been provided for generously in the official plans. Now, however, with evacuation a reality, she found herself forced into battle with all sorts of opportunists eager to displace the creatures for their own profit. Finally, after exhaustive negotiations, it was agreed the animals would travel together by compound with their own caregivers in some old cargo vessels originally set aside for scrap. It was a less than ideal arrangement.

The situation with the ocean dwellers — hundreds of deep ocean creatures and dozens of whales and porpoises — was even more compelling. These creatures were, by their own choosing, untagged, and Deirdre had no way of communicating with them. Air Command refused to free up the

156

hydrofoils necessary for a visual search. Finally, several of the pirates, hearing of her plight, offered to double back for a look after the main evacuation was complete.

Then, as if driven by some anxiety all their own, two of the herring gulls took wing and did not return to the nest. Deirdre had tagged them, but the vehicle necessary for their recovery had been packed in the lead ship with other scientific equipment and had already left for the New Colonies. She plotted the gulls on her map, growing more anxious as the tiny dots grew progressively farther from the nest.

Jaffey and Morgan — she would have been grateful for their companionship if nothing else — were burdened with their own responsibilities. Morgan, with the task of photographing the planet in its final days, answered her notes with the most cryptic responses. Jaffey, after an impassioned audio-video pledging her troth and undying love, was swallowed up in a morass of conflicting duties and obligations. Everyone wanted her attention, from the technicians laboring to meet the increased burdens placed on aging equipment to developers on Zeta Base, quarreling over the fairness of expropriation payments.

Tragedies occurred hourly. Half the books in the library disintegrated when the chambers holding them were decompressed prematurely. Then a guard at the National Gallery failed to properly secure the locks on the special vessel carrying hundreds of ancient paintings to the New Colonies. Everything was lost when the ship jumped to hyperspace.

Throughout those terrible hours, Antiquity stood by her console, trying frantically to key her message into consoles throughout the universe. The transmission systems were clogged. She called for her vehicle and went personally to visit each Union representative. Most of the members had already arrived for the Union Council and had taken rooms at the Grand Hotel. She spoke to them urgently, eloquently, and they heard what she had to say, leaning toward her respectfully, listening intently, their faces pinched with anxiety, their eyes puffed with exhaustion. They were distracted, however, trying in vain to comprehend the mountains of information spewing from their portable computers. They could not make any commitments. Even those sympathetic to her position merely murmured and nodded and held her hand reverently and long. They were paralyzed with fear, rendered impotent by the awesome nature of their burdens. Antiquity left the hotel in despair.

Jaffey was not at the hotel. When Antiquity inquired, she was told Jaffey had gone to Zeta Base to meet with her constituents. Antiquity left messages at every possible location but Jaffey did not respond.

When Antiquity arrived home it was after the dinner hour. Deirdre was in the sanctuary when she arrived. She saw the old woman limping up the path to her quarters, thin and frail and exhausted. She hastily made a pot of tea and carried it to the loft. Antiquity was bent over her console. The abacus lay at her side.

"Did you find Jaffey?" Deirdre asked.

Antiquity turned to her, distraught. Her white hair was frazzled and sticking out in all directions like a great ragged halo.

"No," she said shortly. She returned her attention to the console. "I'm certain this is correct," she muttered. "The probability of probe failure in the location I've keyed in cannot be that high. It's impossible. I've made absolutely exacting adjustments. I've even taken the solar wind factor into consideration. The abacus suggests my hunch is correct but it will take me forever to confirm the figures by hand. I don't have forever." Antiquity began to punch wildly at the console, her long white hair entwining itself in the keys.

"I've brought tea," Deirdre said quietly.

Jaffey and Millgrew arrived at the compound late that evening. The animal sanctuary was a beehive of activity as dozens of workers helped prepare the creatures for the long voyage ahead.

Deirdre was not with the animals. Jaffey stopped briefly at her private quarters then joined Millgrew in the courtyard. Together they climbed the steps to Antiquity's quarters.

Deirdre met them at the door. "Where have you been?" she asked Jaffey. "She's been trying to reach you for hours."

"There is nothing getting through to Zeta Base. I returned just minutes ago. I picked up the message at the airport and came here immediately."

"At least you're here," said Deirdre, relenting. "Antiquity's counting on you, Jaffey. She believes you're the one who can help her." She took Jaffey by the hand. "Come, she's working at her console."

"Jaffey," Antiquity rasped. "At last! This machine

is behaving in the most ridiculous fashion. The figures it suggest for solar probabilities are ludicrous."

"Antiquity," said Jaffey gently, "I've just arrived from Zeta Base. I received your call at the airport and came here directly. I've checked the lists. Arrangements have been made for you and Deirdre on Zeta Base. You'll stay at my home of course. You leave on Thursday. I'm not sure if I will be available —"

"Available!" Antiquity cut Jaffey off abruptly. "What's all this nonsense about Zeta Base? I'm not going anywhere, Jaffey. None of us is. I've reworked my calculations, taking into account the latest shifts in solar activity. With precision —"

Jaffey walked up to Antiquity and, putting a hand on each shoulder, looked directly into her eyes. "Antiquity," she said quietly, "it's over. All that remains is the vote tomorrow and that's a formality."

"What do you mean?" Antiquity took a step backward, stumbling in her anxiety.

"Evacuation is a foregone conclusion. It's the only way. It's the only option left to us. You'll see that when you've had time to reflect."

"Time to reflect!" Antiquity gasped. "What do you think I do all day? What do you think I've thought of every day since I was a small child? The force of the winds off Outer Platenius? I have thought of nothing but Our Mother and her salvation."

"Earth can't be saved," Jaffey said firmly. She looked into Antiquity's face earnestly as if talking to a small child. "We have known for many years that Earth is in a marginal state. That's why we've always had a comprehensive evacuation plan."

160

"Nonsense!" Antiquity grasped Jaffey by the lapels, her bony fingers fluttering uncertainly over the rough fabric. "The evacuation plans are nonsense. They were devised by weaklings and cowards and people without souls, people who talk about Earth as they would discuss a pebble in their shoe." She released Jaffey and turned away, pale and shaken. "Those people were born and reared away from us, Jaffey. They've forgotten what Earth is to us. She's our womb, our conscience. She's everything we are. If we abandon her, we abandon our souls. We will be nothing but parasites, floating through the universe, becoming less than human. The Earth is not expendable, Jaffey. She is all of us who ever were. We can run away. But when she dies, so do we."

Jaffey looked at Millgrew helplessly then turned back to Antiquity. "Come to Zeta Base," she cajoled. "You'll love it. It's Earth reborn, primordial Earth at the time just after the great rains, after the eruption of the giant trees. Green and damp, soggy, filled with misty blue lagoons and splendid inland waterfalls. It sparkles, Antiquity. The sky is as blue as Earth's was at the dawn of time. And bright too, lit by a vigorous new sun. It's the Earth you've always dreamed of."

"It's nothing but a pale copy, plastic and synthetic," cried Antiquity. "Its trees have no life blood. They're plastic to the core. I would never abandon Earth for such a place."

"You have no choice," said Jaffey quietly. "Earth is doomed. Even if we could save her, we can't continue to support her in her present state. The probability of successfully reigniting the sun is less

161

than forty percent. If we make the slightest mistake in our calculations, if we err by the flimsiest of margins we could destroy the solar system. The chances of that happening are nearly fifty percent."

"Your figures are nonsense," cried Antiquity. "Jaffey, a dense nuclear pack aimed at 14.068 solar latitude would accomplish the task at minimal risk, provided we act within the next few days while the solar wind is less than five kph. I have some preliminary figures from my abacus. I have extrapolated from them to arrive at my results. The risk is minimal, much less than we thought. The greatest risk is that nothing will happen at all. Look at my figures, Jaffey, and tell me if you still believe." Antiquity took the sheaf of papers and thrust them forward.

Jaffey shook her head. "Antiquity," she said. "Some of these figures are pure guesswork, the product of your imagination. Hunch. They bear not an iota of resemblance to SOLCOM's solar probabilities."

"SOLCOM's probabilities!" Antiquity glared at Jaffey, enraged. "Marcus Vinkle has manipulated us. He was clever enough to deceive us about the neutrino figures. Have you not considered the possibility that he's manipulated the probabilities as well?" Deflated by the set expression on Jaffey's face, Antiquity pleaded, "At least give me your vote in the Assembly tomorrow. Your vote will give me the three I need to obtain a period of grace to fill in the missing blanks with the hard data you so crave."

"I can't support you, Antiquity."

"What do you mean, you can't support me!"

Antiquity spluttered. "Can't you see the decision to abandon Earth is mainly a political one? You've been hoodwinked! Bamboozled by the worst kind of political chicanery. The colonies have a vested interest in abandoning Earth. Can't you see that? All they consider is the profit line. Earth costs them money. Their taxes go to maintain the greenhouse effect. The President is the creature of the colonies. When the opportunity presented itself, she was happy to seize it. The next thing we know, Marcus Vinkle will be Chief of State. Perhaps even science-philosopher," she added with a bitter laugh. "Will that be his reward for his part in this unholy alliance? If Earth is sacrificed to them to achieve their dreams, what is it to them? By withholding the truth, they have created panic for their own purposes. The people are in a daze. They scarcely know what is happening. They are so concerned with survival, they have neither the will nor the ability to consider my proposal rationally."

Her voice was cracked, dry and broken. She turned away. "What of the President and Marcus Vinkle? They are not of Earth." Antiquity stared hard at Jaffey. "Neither are you," she said, suddenly subdued. "Well, what has she promised you?"

Jaffey's cheeks flamed. She started to speak then turned abruptly and left the room. Millgrew followed.

Deirdre stopped them at the door. "Are you going to help her? You have a ship. You have probe-launching capacity. You have security clearance —"

Jaffey put a hand to Deirdre's mouth to silence her. "I know how devoted you are to Antiquity, but what you propose is treason. It's up to the Council to decide and the Council will vote for evacuation. It's a formality."

"Jaffey," she pleaded, "at least give Antiquity your vote. She has Nadril's. No one would fault you for voting for your old patron. Your vote would give her the three days she so desperately wants. And you would know you've made at least a minimal gesture on her behalf."

Jaffey didn't answer immediately. Instead she took Deirdre into her arms. "Come with me to Zeta Base," she whispered. "Your animals would be free to roam as they did years ago in their natural state. Imagine your big cats leaping in the branches of the willows overhanging the lagoons. Imagine us, lovers, on the grassy banks. I'll see to it arrangements are made exactly as you wish. I'm a Union Counselor, Deirdre," she said earnestly. "I can do these things. I can give you everything you want."

Deirdre looked at Jaffey with pain in her eyes. She said with difficulty, "Give Antiquity your vote. That's all I ask."

Jaffey sighed.

To Jaffey's surprise the pass card worked. Her security clearance had been restored. It would seem SOLCOM had nothing more to hide.

She let the door fall softly behind her and made her way quietly to Marcus's office. She told herself there was no reason to feel guilty. Searching Marcus's office, while rude, did not constitute a breech of ethics for the chief engineer.

She used her card once again to enter Marcus's suite. She took a light from her pocket and tried the door to the inner office. This time her card didn't work. Suddenly every light in the room went on. A dozen uniformed guards appeared in the doorway.

Marcus Vinkle shoved his way to the fore. "Wait outside," he said to the guards. "What are you looking for, Jaffey?"

"The records of solar probabilities," Jaffey said boldly. "I want to make sure I have the latest figures before I cast my vote tomorrow."

"Probabilities," Marcus said with a grin. "Oh, I think you'll find the relevents to be about fifty percent."

"Antiquity thinks the numbers are a great deal lower," said Jaffey pleasantly.

For a moment, Marcus hesitated. "Oh, they are," he said with a sudden grin. "But you'll never prove it."

Jaffey stared at Marcus, incredulous. "Are you saying you deliberately falsified the probability projections?"

Marcus nodded. "I was wondering how long it would take before you got suspicious," he said nonchalantly. "Actually I thought you'd figure it all out much sooner." He shook his head. "Everyone's so trusting, Jaffey. Except Antiquity."

"How did you do it?"

Marcus shrugged. "It was ridiculously simple," he said brightly. "I infected the computer bank with a very selective and undetectable virus. There's no independent source of verification. Except Antiquity's ancient bead game. But who would put any faith in that? With you tied up in the transit project, it was easy." Marcus's eyes opened wide. "You wouldn't believe how gullible people are, Jaffey. No one makes inquiries. If it comes out of a machine, they believe it."

Jaffey crossed her arms. "What is the truth then? What are the probabilities?"

Marcus stroked his chin, thoughtfully. "Well, the probability of Antiquity's scheme succeeding is about fifty percent. The probability of a catastrophic explosion occurring is tiny, probably even smaller than Antiquity has predicted. It's most unlikely any of the space stations would be affected."

"Then it's entirely feasible to evacuate the population and explode a probe."

"Entirely," Marcus said cheerfully. "Oh, we might experience a minor heat wave at first but nothing much else. You must remember too, all earlier projections were based on a fuller sun."

"And the President went along with this?"

Marcus grinned. "She doesn't know anything about the virus. She acted like a politician, but that's her only crime. As far as she knows, she's come clean."

Jaffey's heart sank. Struggling to maintain her composure, she glanced toward the shadows of the guards looming outside the frosted panes. "Why?"

Marcus shrugged. "Power. When the dust settles, there'll be a huge power vacuum. With the President — but mostly," he continued quickly, "it was for revenge. I would have done it for that alone."

Jaffey stared at Marcus, bewildered. "I don't understand."

"Hasn't Antiquity told you the story of R-11?"

Jaffey shook her head, uncomprehending. "R-11

166

was a tiny asteroid in the Orphus Complex, Maglion Chain. It was force-mined for cruelite some years ago."

"R-11 was my home," said Marcus savagely. "Don't you see, Jaffey? Antiquity made the decision to destroy R-11. It was her responsibility." He turned away, his face dark with fury. "I can't wait to see the expression on the old woman's face tomorrow when the vote is taken and she knows she is truly defeated."

He began to pace the room excitedly. "I'll be glad when it's over, Jaffey. It's been a strain. Everything's so precise at this level. The difference between triumph and disaster is so minute. I'm smarter than the others. So much smarter. You're the only one who's smarter than I. Still it's been a strain. I don't know what I would have done if you hadn't been preoccupied with the transit initiative. If you'd been prying into my affairs on a daily basis — as it was, from the minute I heard you were coming — I must confess, I quaked a bit inside —"

Marcus was eager to tell his story. "When I first discovered the problem, I went strictly by the book. I took only the President into my confidence. At first, we delayed simply because we were so shocked. We couldn't believe what was going on. Then we had to confirm data and design projections." Marcus paused, wiping his brow. "You wouldn't believe how long it takes for one person to calculate the effects of a probe, scarcely forty megacones, striking a discreet spot on the sun with shifting heat and wind determinants."

Marcus's face hardened. "Then Antiquity came on the scene with her primitive neutrino counter. She

167

was a bit behind me but not much. It embarrasses me to admit how close she came with that rickety instrument. When I saw how frantic she was, when I realized how huge her stake was personally, I couldn't resist. She had that look in her eye my adoptive mother had when she told me R-11 was dead. I remember that day well." Marcus flushed deep red as he said this and the veins stood out ominously on his forehead.

"Revenge," said Jaffey quietly. "A monstrous hoax purely for revenge."

Marcus took a deep breath. "At first it was a game. I embellished it for my own amusement. It grew from there. Finally, it got out of hand — the game, the deception. I couldn't stop even if I had wanted to. There was no turning back."

Jaffey caught a glimmer of hope. "You could have stopped anytime, Marcus. You could stop even now. So far, no harm's been done. No one's been hurt."

"No!" Marcus turned away. "They'd exile me to some remote place, strip me of my property, my accomplishments. No. This is my chance to get to the top, to gain respect."

Marcus paused, gathering his composure. "Do you know what gauche means, Jaffey? Clumsy. Not sophisticated enough. Ugly. I've heard them laugh behind my back. If it hadn't been for Ludmilla, for her intervention, I would still be a junior officer, scarcely more than a technician in spite of my brilliance. So, that's it, Jaffey. I can't stop now."

"What then?"

"Antiquity will die. I'll become science-philosopher. President. Even Chief Engineer. Whatever I want."

Jaffey took a deep breath. "And me? Do you plan to kill me too?"

For a moment, Marcus looked troubled. "Well, not right away. I need your creativity, your intellect. I have something else in mind."

Jaffey awoke on a table, an electronic cap covering her head.

"Think of some moments you valued," a voice told her. "Think of your feelings. You may not experience them again."

Jaffey squeezed her eyes together, desperate. She thought of home — Zeta Base, bright and sparkling in the sunlight. She saw Antiquity, grave and dignified, surrounded by her flock of eager white-robed moppets. The Academy. Tristan. Then her mind cleared. She was on the beach with Deirdre, rolling over and over in the white sand.

Her mind went black.

Chapter 13

Deirdre came to Antiquity's quarters two hours before the Council was to meet. She woke her and, while she washed, prepared a breakfast of coffee and whole-grain bread.

Antiquity took a small vessel of icy water to her bedroom. There, she removed her robe and washed her face and chest, gasping slightly as the cold water produced a painful contraction in her pectoral muscles. Her breasts were small shriveled sacs, scarcely distinguishable from the multiplicity of loose desiccated folds of tissue that comprised her chest.

She dried herself and put on the clean robe Deirdre had put out for her.

Her body smelled mildly antiseptic and felt brittle, as if she had been bathed in formaldehyde. She parted her flowing hair carefully at the center and brushed it so that it fell behind each ear. The hair was a symbol of maturity and wisdom.

She took her breakfast on the balcony. She sat and stared gloomily out over the water, barely touching her food. The sun seemed brighter today than ever before, shimmering off the bay, mocking her with its deceitful display of good health. She took a small sip of coffee, then with a sudden sob in her heart, choked and was forced to set the beverage aside.

When it came time to leave for the Assembly Building, Deirdre insisted upon accompanying her. Antiquity knew Deirdre was hard-pressed to meet her own obligations but she protested only weakly. She needed her. Her presence was a symbol of her faith.

"There is nothing to worry about," Antiquity said as Deirdre prepared to take her seat in the gallery. "I need only three votes to force a review. If I am given time, I am certain I can rally the people to my side. Nadril will be with me. She is confirmed. Jaffey is confirmed. She promised you. She will support me out of loyalty if nothing else."

Nadril sat dozing over her briefing papers. Antiquity looked at her, despairing. She felt lost and forlorn, having forgotten her own notes. Then she assured herself she would remember whatever she needed to remember and relaxed.

The remaining counselors arrived, murmuring

171

among themselves. They were not on her side and it embarrassed them to look into her eyes.

Jaffey arrived at the last moment and took her seat at the rear of the Hall. She did not look at Antiquity but stared straight ahead at her desk. Marcus Vinkle accompanied her to the floor, then strolled boldly to the front of the room and took a seat in the section reserved for appointed advisors.

The President entered the room just as the chimes of the last bell died away. She looked very tired. At last the Hall was quiet.

The President cleared her throat. "You have received copies of our evacuation schedules. You have had the opportunity to meet with your constituents and with each other to give information and share opinions."

The President droned on. Antiquity sat, head bowed, thinking of the plans for the probe that lay on her desk at home.

"We will proceed with the vote without further ado," said the President abruptly. "All those in favor."

There was a brief flurry of activity as the votes were registered. In ancient ceremony, the sergeant at arms weaved between the aisles, noting each vote and marking it against the name on his master seating plan.

"All opposed?" said the President.

Antiquity raised her hand, turning at the same time to look at Nadril. The old woman gazed at Antiquity, her eyes bleary.

"Vote!" whispered Antiquity angrily.

Nadril raised her hand obligingly.

Antiquity turned back with a sigh, her hands trembling slightly.

The sergeant at arms entered the vote and passed the master list to the President.

"The vote is official," said the President gravely.

A great hush fell over the Hall. Antiquity sat, staring at her hands. The silence seemed to go on for hours. She waited in a vacuum of timelessness, awaiting the President's instructions. She moved her lips as she waited, rehearsing what the President would say. *The vote stands negative at three. The Counselors are instructed to return to their constituents for three more days of study and discussion. The Council is now recessed.*

"I hesitate to leave you without a few words," said the President. "It is impossible to grasp the enormity of what we have done. I fear, at this time, we can do little more than bear intellectual witness —"

Antiquity sat forward suddenly, as if struck. The blood rushed to her cheeks, then drained away. She stood, gasped, then collapsed back into her chair.

"Antiquity!" Deirdre hurried down from the gallery as the old woman clawed at the security guards who had thrown a cordon around the Chief Engineer.

Deirdre turned toward Jaffey, ashen. Marcus Vinkle stepped quickly between them, shielding Jaffey from Deirdre's vision.

"Regrets to Antiquity," murmured Marcus. He steered Jaffey from the chambers.

Chapter 14

Over the next two days, the evacuation proceeded apace. By noon of the second day, fifty thousand people had been lifted to temporary shelter in the New Colonies.

Throughout this time, Antiquity worked feverishly, transmitting her messages throughout the planet. But, increasingly, as the hours passed, her efforts went for naught. Consoles, for the most part, were logged to emergency addresses.

By noon of the third day, Antiquity had abandoned her console and went on foot to the town square. There, with only a few souls to listen, she ranted until dusk.

A friend of Deirdre's took her aside and, in a low voice, said, "Nadril has disappeared. Her friends tell me she is ill. They look frightened when they talk about her. I feel uneasy talking to you. Antiquity is in grave danger. If you want to save her, silence her."

Deirdre watched Antiquity closely, her concern deepening as the hours passed. Antiquity sat on her chair all night, smiling to herself and, occasionally, laughing out loud. Deirdre tried unsuccessfully to contact Delphi.

When the first sliver of light broke the darkness, Deirdre went to the kitchen to prepare coffee. Antiquity continued to sit cross-legged on her pillow, drawing her tongue over lips that were now dry and crusted. Deirdre knew Antiquity had not eaten since the morning of the Union Council. She had taken only fluids and those sparingly.

Rumor had it — a rumor reluctantly confirmed by Millgrew — that Jaffey had moved into the President's quarters. Deirdre's attempts to reach her there, however, proved futile. Deirdre knew Jaffey could be inconsiderate at times but never cold and insensitive.

She returned to Antiquity, bathed her and put her to bed. Then she closed the door quietly and went out into the living room.

Suddenly Jaffey was in the room, standing at one end of the long corridor.

"Jaffey, you're here." She laughed with relief. She ran toward Jaffey, her arms wide open. Suddenly she stopped, paralyzed by the expressionless face and vacant eyes. "Jaffey?"

"There's no need to wake her." Jaffey stepped forward, flung Deirdre from her and began to move down the hall. "Take me to the old woman," she said mechanically.

"No!" Deirdre ran after Jaffey, grabbing at her wrist.

A knife clattered to the floor between them. "Get out of my way," Jaffey hissed, "or I will kill you too."

Deirdre lunged for the knife but moments later she knew the fight was over. Blood trickled down her face, her right wrist hung limp at her side. The knuckles of the left were slashed and bleeding. Deirdre struggled to her feet, holding the wrist against her breast.

Jaffey raised the knife.

"Jaffey," she whispered, "it's Deirdre. Deirdre."

The knife stood poised inches from her chest. There was a strange lupine wavering in the eyes. Deirdre ducked. The knife slammed into the wall, embedding itself. Jaffey fell back, her hand oozing blood. She stood, staring at it. Then, suddenly, she turned and fled.

Morgan Quade squinted to see through the narrow slit in the cell door. Technicians scurried about, laden with boxes of software and the disassembled carcasses of hardware. She began to beat against the door, hoping to attract the attention of the guard. Finally she put her boot through the surveillance eye.

Within seconds a guard appeared at the doorway, motioning to her to stand back.

"I have a right to contact three people," Morgan told him. "What penal code am I held under? Will I be put to death or will I simply be lobotomized?"

Marcus Vinkle appeared suddenly in the doorway. He said lightly, "We wouldn't put you to death, Morgan Quade. Capital punishment is no longer part of the code. We merely remove the parts of your brain responsible for the aberrant, harmful behavior."

Her eyes dissected him. "I see."

He shrugged. "Perhaps we could even make me more appealing to you. Perhaps that could be done."

"I doubt that very much." She took a step toward him, arms folded.

The look in her eyes made him giggle nervously. "I've always had an eye for you, Morgan," he blurted out. "I've always been curious to know what you're —"

Morgan stepped forward quickly, raising one knee with full force. Marcus collapsed to the floor, writhing. The guard rushed in, tripped over Marcus's prostate form, lost his balance. Morgan grabbed his gun and ran, slamming the door behind her.

Deirdre was not in the sanctuary, nor in her apartment either. Morgan ran across the compound and up the steps to Antiquity's loft.

The door was wide open. There was blood

everywhere. Morgan stepped across the threshold, eyes widening at the knife embedded in the wall like Excalibur.

"Deirdre," she called softly.

"Morgan, I'm here."

Morgan ran to the balcony. Deirdre lay near the bench, one eye swollen shut. Blood crusted her lips and matted her hair. One wrist seeped blood, the knuckles on one hand were enlarged and bruised.

"It was Jaffey," Deirdre said with difficulty. "She came here to kill Antiquity."

"Are you all right?" Morgan said, palpating the wounds gently.

Deirdre held up the wrist. "This is the worst. Jaffey was like a stranger," she continued hoarsely. "She behaved as though she barely knew me."

Morgan reached for the communicator and called the sanctuary. "Medical aid," she said quickly. "Antiquity's quarters." She took Deirdre in her arms and held her in a long, tender embrace, releasing her with great reluctance. "Listen carefully," she said at last. "I don't have time to explain but don't trust Marcus Vinkle or anyone acting in his name. They've lied to everyone all along — about everything."

"Then, Antiquity was right —"

"Yes." Morgan glanced about anxiously. "I have to go now," she said quickly. "They'll be looking for their vehicle and I don't want them to find it here."

"I'm going with you."

"No, stay here. I need you here. Find a safe place for us. If we're caught together, I'll have no one to rely on." She started at the sound of a foot on the stairs. "It's medical aid," she said with relief. "I'll leave by the back door. Don't tell anyone I was here."

She kissed Deirdre and then she was gone.

Jaffey leapt from her land vehicle and raced across the tarmac to her ship. The runways were flooded. Great Union vessels swept majestically to the flight deck, hatches open, ready to receive passengers for the New Colonies.

Jaffey saw none of this. Her Tach special was idling at the end of the runway, just as Marcus Vinkle said it would be. Opening the hatch, she took her helmet from the pilot's seat, then stood, staring at the gleaming dashboard. The vessel raised nothing in her yet, intellectually, she thought it should. She had built it herself. She knew that. About to step into the vessel, she heard someone call her name.

She turned to see Morgan Quade running toward her dressed in khaki fatigues and over them an old flight suit, unzippered at the throat and leggings. She clutched her camera bag. Six feet from the vessel, she stopped suddenly, pulling a stun gun from her pocket.

"Get in and be quick about it." Morgan tossed the camera bag into the navigator's seat and pushed Jaffey roughly into the cockpit.

Morgan stared at Jaffey, her eyes narrowed. "Take off your helmet," she said.

Jaffey obeyed.

The vacant eyes made Morgan's blood run cold. She ran one hand gently through Jaffey's hair, searching, trying to avoid the lifeless gaze.

"What have they done to you?" she whispered. "Lobotomy? No. They haven't shaved you and there are no scorch marks." She held the gun tightly to Jaffey's side, her hand smoothing the hair along Jaffey's temples. "They shocked you," she said angrily. "What did they do then? Brainwash you? Program you to seek out and kill Antiquity? Now what?"

"I'm to go to Zeta Base and assassinate the President," Jaffey said without blinking an eye.

Morgan looked at Jaffey, pained, then said tightly, "They'll kill you when they're done with you." She took a deep breath. "Let's get going. Here are your new coordinates." She reached past Jaffey and slid the map into the autonavigator. "We're launching a probe."

"We couldn't possibly eject in time," Jaffey said mechanically. "Even if we could, our ejection capsules would probably explode."

Morgan slammed the gun hard into Jaffey's ribs. "In two minutes," she said clearly, "Marcus Vinkle's men will be all over the tarmac. If I go back I'm dead. Dead or some mindless concubine for Marcus Vinkle."

Jaffey stared at her blankly.

"The very best I have to look forward to is life as a blind artist, Jaffey," she said bitterly. "An artist with someone else's eyes. I would rather be blind, I think. If I'm going to go, I'm going in a blaze of glory."

Morgan's transmission began as a single dot of brilliant color on Alf's console. The dot expanded rapidly, exploding into a vibrant flood of colors, images and artistic impressions.

The editor leaned forward, open-mouthed. "Where is she?" he whispered to himself.

Even as he spoke, images of greater intensity and artistic wizardry emerged. The colors were dazzling — scorching reds and oranges, touched rarely but dramatically with swatches of dense black and flickering gaseous blue. And through the colors ran the razor's edge of human emotion, startling images of joy and pain.

Alf stared at the screen, his peripheral awareness fast fading. He was sucked inexorably into the fiery pit, led there by the master. His mind received but could not comprehend. He felt at once hot and cold, at once unchaste and purified. He was, for one brief moment, the victor and the vanquished. Then, with a terrible explosion, the images melded. He saw it all and understood everything.

Delphi Norbert was about to leave the dispensary when the call came through. The shuttle pilot came in at a low angle and darted to a stop on the sparse brown field to the left of the rose garden. The medic scrambled out, and with the help of the pilot, pulled a stretcher from the cargo bay. Together they ran toward the dispensary.

Delphi met them at the door, motioning them quickly toward the surgery. She bent over the capsule, her fingers working nervously at the seals.

"We left the seals intact," the medic explained quickly. "We were afraid the body might disintegrate." The medic found the terminals and began to clip them into the charred debris.

Delphi took the tracing and touched the computer match with trembling fingers. She gasped and dropped the probe. "My God," she said, her voice quavering, "it's Morgan." She shook her head resolutely. There was no time for tears.

Millgrew burst through the door of Delphi's waiting room just as Delphi emerged from the surgery. "I took everything available from the first-aid kits at the Academy," said Millgrew. She grabbed Delphi's arm. "Where is she?"

Delphi pointed to what appeared to be a blanket bundle on the bench in the corner. "You'll wake Deirdre. I've given her a sedative. A groundskeeper brought her here with her hand dangling by a thread."

"I must see Morgan," Millgrew insisted. "She would know what happened to Jaffey."

"I assume she vaporized." Delphi stared at Millgrew, taken aback. "She must have. Morgan is barely —"

"I must see her." Millgrew slipped past Delphi. She crossed the floor of the dispensary in a few quick strides, pushed open the door of the surgery, then stopped dead in her tracks.

"Please don't look at me." Morgan's husky voice came out a low, robot's growl.

Millgrew looked away, tearful. "I need to know," she whispered. She stared hard at the wall, blinking back tears furiously. "When did you see her last? Did you eject at the same time?"

"No —" Morgan's words ended in a scream of pain.

"It's all right, dear," said Delphi, distressed. "Just whisper."

There was a long painful pause. Straining to hear, Delphi leaned over Morgan, her eyes glistening. Finally she straightened, moved away from the cot and pulled the curtains around it.

"She says she ejected Jaffey's capsule as soon as she was certain she no longer needed manual pilot. She stayed with the ship for several more minutes then ejected."

"But why would she stay?"

"Who knows?"

"Then Jaffey is alive," said Millgrew, her eyes brightening with hope. "She's orbiting, awaiting rescue."

"Oh, Millgrew, I don't think —"

Millgrew was already out the door.

Antiquity stood back from the threshold, inviting Millgrew to enter. She wore a fresh robe of the palest blue and in her hand carried a beverage pure and festive. "I'm pleased you have come of course but I would have expected a visit from the President or, at the very least, from Marcus Vinkle."

"I have come to tell you Jaffey is missing," Millgrew said painfully, "and to urge you to leave this place with me. I have made arrangements."

Antiquity went on as if she hadn't heard. "It's a glorious day, Millgrew," she said. "My theories were correct. The neutrino level has responded exactly as I predicted. I expect it will increase at a safe, steady rate until the planet is restored. I knew Jaffey would not let me down. However she accomplished this, I'm anxious to hear the details."

"Morgan Quade is near death and unlikely to survive," Millgrew said quietly.

"If the ozone and thermal effects are properly regulated, we should realize Earth's ante-maunder environment within the decade without damaging critical balances."

Millgrew stepped toward Antiquity. "Our situation is critical," she said urgently. "Rumors abound. The President is said to be a virtual prisoner on Zeta Base. Marcus Vinkle is drunk with power. The word is he has gathered a group of technicians and guards and has stockpiled scores of dense pack nuclear projectiles at critical points with the purpose of solidifying his control. It's only a matter of time before they come for you, Antiquity. I have called in my debts at the Academy to secure a private vessel. If we hurry we may be able to escape under the cover of confusion."

Antiquity stared at Millgrew, brows knit uncertainly. "You say Jaffey is missing?" Her voice was small and childlike.

"Morgan is near death, and you are in grave danger, as am I. I will attempt to reach the frontier. We should find safety there — at least temporarily.

I'm praying we can make contact with a friendly vessel."

The old woman took a long breath. The sound reminded Millgrew of the creaks and sighs of wind passing through the shrubland.

"Then I must say goodbye to this place," Antiquity said finally. "I —"

Antiquity's words were lost in a commotion from the courtyard. Millgrew ran to the balcony and looked down. The courtyard was swarming with Union vehicles. One bore the seal of the President.

"They're here for us."

A strange look crossed the old woman's face. "There's a way out," she said. "A small balcony off my bedroom leads to the cliff from the railing."

Millgrew nodded, then froze.

Antiquity teetered on the balcony over the courtyard, arms outstretched.

"Stay back," said Antiquity hoarsely. "I'll never leave this place. I'll distract them to let you get safely away."

"No!"

"My body is with Earth," Antiquity intoned.

For a moment the frail figure steadied. Then Antiquity was gone. Millgrew heard a small cry. Then silence. The wind whipped the curtains lightly.

A whistle blew in the courtyard. The blast was followed by an excited garble of voices.

"Antiquity!"

Millgrew ran to the bedroom and onto the tiny balcony. She vaulted over the edge, and disappeared over the cliff.

* * * * *

Morgan was awake. "Delphi?" The growl was weaker.

"Yes, yes, I'm here." Delphi leaned over Morgan.

The anxiety in the voice disappeared into a choking laugh. "My head is itchy — whatever you're doing — I want to scratch it — but I don't know if I have a hand."

"It's all right." Delphi turned to the oscilloscope.

"Those flashes of light — mostly in my mind — really nothing — like my hand — it's not really there — I can feel it."

Delphi stared at the oscilloscope for a moment then completed the hook-up. "There," she muttered, "that's it. Morgan —" she touched the stretcher — "Morgan, I have it. It's working. I can do it."

Morgan emitted a strangled cough. "The headache is terrible."

"Oh, it's just the chemical wastes building up. You can handle it. Morgan," she said clearly, "I'm going to move you. It's going to work. You'll be whole."

"New eyes?"

"Yes, yes, new eyes too."

"Good, because I'm blind now. There's nothing. I'm smiling. Can you see?"

"Yes," said Delphi, distressed, "I can see you smile. We're going over, Morgan," she said firmly. "You'll have to concentrate. I need your help."

Delphi watched the pattern of the oscilloscope.

Delphi teetered back on her heels for a moment, her face damp with perspiration. "Now," she said, swallowing hard, "we're going on a great journey."

186

There was a great silence, then Morgan said with startling clarity, "Delphi, I'm dying."

Deirdre paced the floor of the waiting room, her stomach on edge from the bitter coffee, her eyes dry and painful. It was very late and she had not slept in some time. She had the empty dull feeling of insomnia and grief.

Day was breaking when the surgery door finally opened. Delphi, devouring the fresh air in great, greedy gulps, took Deirdre's hand in hers and led her into the surgery.

A small box covered with a thick white cloth lay on the table in the surgery. Deirdre stiffened.

"Don't look at that," said Delphi quickly. "There's nothing there. Surgical debris." She motioned Deirdre into the infirmary behind the surgery.

The room was shaded and quiet. Three cots stood against the opposite wall, one enveloped in curtains. Delphi put a finger to her lips and pulled the curtains aside.

Morgan lay on the cot, naked under a thin sheet. She looked as fresh and dewy as a lamb just born, fresh from its mother's licking.

Deirdre stared. "Morgan," she said hoarsely.

"Yes, it's Morgan." Delphi pulled the sheet gently over the exposed breast. "It was the most amazing thing, Deirdre," Delphi whispered. "Absolutely amazing. I watched her move from one to the other. First, an impulse on my oscilloscope. Then a profound silence. Something passing. Almost brushing my skin — like a breeze, a soft, warm breeze. Then, I looked into her eyes and there she was. I watched her appear in her eyes." Delphi shook her head as if dazed. "And then she fell asleep. Exhausted, I suppose. Me too."

The door in the outer office opened. Delphi turned with a start. She pulled the curtain quickly and stepped out. Marcus Vinkle stood at the entrance to the surgery, flanked by several guards.

"I came to express my sympathies, Delphi," he said, "at the passing of our friend Jaffey. My intelligence tells me her Mach 5 was lost."

"Your sympathies are accepted," said Delphi coolly.

"Yes." Marcus cleared his throat and said, "I understand there was a passenger."

"Yes." Delphi put her hands into her pockets crisply. "Morgan Quade." She picked up the file and handed it to him.

"And?"

"She's dead," Delphi said bleakly. "She lived only a few hours and never regained consciousness. I've just finished the paperwork."

"Yes." Marcus stared at the record, slightly taken aback.

"Her body is here," said Delphi. She drew the cotton shroud aside and opened the lid of the box. "There," she said calmly. "There are the remains. They're yours if you want them, Marcus."

Marcus's face turned red. He put a hand to his throat. "No need," he said weakly. "Please release them as you wish."

"The death certificate is here," said Delphi mildly. "I have already filed a copy with central."

Delphi watched until the vehicle pulled away, then returned to the infirmary. Morgan was sleeping peacefully. Deirdre sat beside her, scarcely daring to breathe. Delphi glanced at the monitor.

"The brain waves show alpha frequency," said Delphi. "She should wake any second. We can only hope."

Morgan's eyelids fluttered.

"She looks so pale," said Deirdre. "I've never seen her so pale."

"This is probably the first time since she was an infant that she hasn't born the mark of some escapade," said Delphi proudly.

Deirdre took Morgan's hand in hers. It was warm and soft. She held it, stroking the fingers gently.

Suddenly the fingers circled hers. Morgan's eyes opened wide. Deirdre stepped back, startled. The eyes stared at her blankly.

"Are you all right?" Delphi leaned forward anxiously.

"Yes." Morgan looked at Delphi for a moment, then winked and said, "But I do have a hell of a hangover." She pulled Deirdre to her and held her in a long tender-rough embrace. "I'm so tired," she whispered. "I'd love to fall asleep holding you."

"There's no time, I'm afraid." Delphi quickly unhooked the monitor as she spoke. "Once Marcus Vinkle gets over the shock, he'll be back to ask questions." She handed two robes to Deirdre. "We're going to Ganda," she said. "There's nothing there but rocks and moss and a few hermits who have taken a

189

vow of silence. We'll be safe there. I've arranged passage for you on a private vessel. The pirate Am says she owes you a favor, Morgan. She'll be here any minute."

"Has Antiquity been sent for?" Deirdre asked anxiously. "She'll go with us, of course."

"Millgrew's looking after her," Delphi assured her. "She's secured a vessel."

"And what about you?" Deirdre helped Morgan with her robe as she spoke.

"I'll join you later." She pulled the robe over Morgan's head. "There, you look like any other hermit rock scientist."

A soft whoosh announced the arrival of the pirate vessel. It hung at the edge of the precipice, extending a short thick plank across the void.

Delphi pushed open the rear door and whisked them outside. Telda Am marched down the plank and stopped at the edge of the precipice, cigar clenched between her teeth, her flight jacket open at the front.

She held out a hand to Morgan. "Good to see you, Quade."

"Have you heard any news?" Delphi asked.

Telda shifted the cigar to the side of her mouth. "Your scrawny friend Millgrew from Sub-Oceana escaped," she said. "We unscrambled that off local Union frequency. Vinkle's in control at present. He's got all the firepower. We'll hightail it to the frontier and mount the resistance from there."

"Marcus has nuclear projectiles," said Delphi unhappily.

"And we've got the moxy," said Telda. "Not to mention the guts." She glanced at her chronometer.

"OK, let's get out of here." She stepped forward and scooped Deirdre into her arms. "Let me help you, little lady. The plank's not too steady." She cast a short glance at Morgan. "You can walk, Quade."

Morgan took Delphi into her arms and gave her a big hug.

"How can I thank you, Delphi?"

"By staying alive until I see you again. Soon, I hope."

"Soon." Morgan released Delphi and turned toward the ship. "It's an adventure, Delphi. Maybe the greatest."

Delphi smiled and shook her head. "Until Ganda," she said softly. She watched as Morgan climbed aboard, watched as the plank was withdrawn and the hatch closed. The ship darted away. Delphi turned toward the surgery.

"Until Ganda."

A few of the publications of
THE NAIAD PRESS, INC.
P.O. Box 10543 • Tallahassee, Florida 32302
Phone (904) 539-5965
Mail orders welcome. Please include 15% postage.

ZETA BASE by Judith Alguire. 208 pp. Lesbian triangle
on a future Earth.   ISBN 0-941483-94-0 $9.95

SECOND CHANCE by Jackie Calhoun. 256 pp. Contemporary
Lesbian lives and loves.   ISBN 0-941483-93-2   9.95

MURDER BY TRADITION by Katherine V. Forrest. 288 pp.
A Kate Delafield Mystery. 4th in a series. ISBN 0-941483-89-4   18.95

BENEDICTION by Diane Salvatore. 272 pp. Striking,
contemporary romantic novel.   ISBN 0-941483-90-8   9.95

CALLING RAIN by Karen Marie Christa Minns. 240 pp.
Spellbinding, erotic love story   ISBN 0-941483-87-8   9.95

BLACK IRIS by Jeane Harris. 192 pp. Caroline's hidden past . . .
                                      ISBN 0-941483-68-1   8.95

TOUCHWOOD by Karin Kallmaker. 240 pp. Loving, May/
December romance.   ISBN 0-941483-76-2   8.95

BAYOU CITY SECRETS by Deborah Powell. 224 pp. A Hollis
Carpenter mystery. First in a series. ISBN 0-941483-91-6   8.95

COP OUT by Claire McNab. 208 pp. 4th Det. Insp. Carol Ashton
mystery.   ISBN 0-941483-84-3   8.95

LODESTAR by Phyllis Horn. 224 pp. Romantic, fast-moving
adventure.   ISBN 0-941483-83-5   8.95

THE BEVERLY MALIBU by Katherine V. Forrest. 288 pp. A
Kate Delafield Mystery. 3rd in a series. (HC) ISBN 0-941483-47-9   16.95
                             Paperback ISBN 0-941483-48-7   9.95

THAT OLD STUDEBAKER by Lee Lynch. 272 pp. Andy's affair
with Regina and her attachment to her beloved car.
                                      ISBN 0-941483-82-7   9.95

PASSION'S LEGACY by Lori Paige. 224 pp. Sarah is swept into
the arms of Augusta Pym in this delightful historical romance.
                                      ISBN 0-941483-81-9   8.95

THE PROVIDENCE FILE by Amanda Kyle Williams. 256 pp.
Second espionage thriller featuring lesbian agent Madison McGuire
                                      ISBN 0-941483-92-4   8.95

I LEFT MY HEART by Jaye Maiman. 320 pp. A Robin Miller
Mystery. First in a series.   ISBN 0-941483-72-X   9.95

THE PRICE OF SALT by Patricia Highsmith (writing as Claire
Morgan). 288 pp. Classic lesbian novel, first issued in 1952 . . .
acknowledged by its author under her own, very famous, name.
ISBN 1-56280-003-5   8.95

SIDE BY SIDE by Isabel Miller. 256 pp. From beloved author of
Patience and Sarah.   ISBN 0-941483-77-0   8.95

SOUTHBOUND by Sheila Ortiz Taylor. 240 pp. Hilarious sequel
to *Faultline.*   ISBN 0-941483-78-9   8.95

STAYING POWER: LONG TERM LESBIAN COUPLES
by Susan E. Johnson. 352 pp. Joys of coupledom.
ISBN 0-941-483-75-4   12.95

SLICK by Camarin Grae. 304 pp. Exotic, erotic adventure.
ISBN 0-941483-74-6   9.95

NINTH LIFE by Lauren Wright Douglas. 256 pp. A Caitlin
Reece mystery. 2nd in a series.   ISBN 0-941483-50-9   8.95

PLAYERS by Robbi Sommers. 192 pp. Sizzling, erotic novel.
ISBN 0-941483-73-8   8.95

MURDER AT RED ROOK RANCH by Dorothy Tell. 224 pp.
First Poppy Dillworth adventure.   ISBN 0-941483-80-0   8.95

LESBIAN SURVIVAL MANUAL by Rhonda Dicksion.
112 pp. Cartoons!   ISBN 0-941483-71-1   8.95

A ROOM FULL OF WOMEN by Elisabeth Nonas. 256 pp.
Contemporary Lesbian lives.   ISBN 0-941483-69-X   8.95

MURDER IS RELATIVE by Karen Saum. 256 pp. The first
Brigid Donovan mystery.   ISBN 0-941483-70-3   8.95

PRIORITIES by Lynda Lyons 288 pp. Science fiction with
a twist.   ISBN 0-941483-66-5   8.95

THEME FOR DIVERSE INSTRUMENTS by Jane Rule. 208
pp. Powerful romantic lesbian stories.   ISBN 0-941483-63-0   8.95

LESBIAN QUERIES by Hertz & Ertman. 112 pp. The questions
you were too embarrassed to ask.   ISBN 0-941483-67-3   8.95

CLUB 12 by Amanda Kyle Williams. 288 pp. Espionage thriller
featuring a lesbian agent!   ISBN 0-941483-64-9   8.95

DEATH DOWN UNDER by Claire McNab. 240 pp. 3rd Det.
Insp. Carol Ashton mystery.   ISBN 0-941483-39-8   8.95

MONTANA FEATHERS by Penny Hayes. 256 pp. Vivian and
Elizabeth find love in frontier Montana.   ISBN 0-941483-61-4   8.95

CHESAPEAKE PROJECT by Phyllis Horn. 304 pp. Jessie &
Meredith in perilous adventure.   ISBN 0-941483-58-4   8.95

LIFESTYLES by Jackie Calhoun. 224 pp. Contemporary Lesbian
lives and loves.   ISBN 0-941483-57-6   8.95

VIRAGO by Karen Marie Christa Minns. 208 pp. Darsen has
chosen Ginny.   ISBN 0-941483-56-8   8.95

WILDERNESS TREK by Dorothy Tell. 192 pp. Six women on
vacation learning "new" skills.   ISBN 0-941483-60-6   8.95

MURDER BY THE BOOK by Pat Welch. 256 pp. A Helen
Black Mystery. First in a series.   ISBN 0-941483-59-2   8.95

BERRIGAN by Vicki P. McConnell. 176 pp. Youthful Lesbian —
romantic, idealistic Berrigan.   ISBN 0-941483-55-X   8.95

LESBIANS IN GERMANY by Lillian Faderman & B. Eriksson.
128 pp. Fiction, poetry, essays.   ISBN 0-941483-62-2   8.95

THERE'S SOMETHING I'VE BEEN MEANING TO TELL
YOU Ed. by Loralee MacPike. 288 pp. Gay men and lesbians
coming out to their children.   ISBN 0-941483-44-4   9.95
                                           ISBN 0-941483-54-1   16.95

LIFTING BELLY by Gertrude Stein. Ed. by Rebecca Mark. 104
pp. Erotic poetry.   ISBN 0-941483-51-7   8.95
                                           ISBN 0-941483-53-3   14.95

ROSE PENSKI by Roz Perry. 192 pp. Adult lovers in a long-term
relationship.   ISBN 0-941483-37-1   8.95

AFTER THE FIRE by Jane Rule. 256 pp. Warm, human novel
by this incomparable author.   ISBN 0-941483-45-2   8.95

SUE SLATE, PRIVATE EYE by Lee Lynch. 176 pp. The gay
folk of Peacock Alley are *all cats.*   ISBN 0-941483-52-5   8.95

CHRIS by Randy Salem. 224 pp. Golden oldie. Handsome Chris
and her adventures.   ISBN 0-941483-42-8   8.95

THREE WOMEN by March Hastings. 232 pp. Golden oldie. A
triangle among wealthy sophisticates.   ISBN 0-941483-43-6   8.95

RICE AND BEANS by Valeria Taylor. 232 pp. Love and
romance on poverty row.   ISBN 0-941483-41-X   8.95

PLEASURES by Robbi Sommers. 204 pp. Unprecedented
eroticism.   ISBN 0-941483-49-5   8.95

EDGEWISE by Camarin Grae. 372 pp. Spellbinding
adventure.   ISBN 0-941483-19-3   9.95

FATAL REUNION by Claire McNab. 224 pp. 2nd Det. Inspec.
Carol Ashton mystery.   ISBN 0-941483-40-1   8.95

KEEP TO ME STRANGER by Sarah Aldridge. 372 pp. Romance
set in a department store dynasty.   ISBN 0-941483-38-X   9.95

HEARTSCAPE by Sue Gambill. 204 pp. American lesbian in
Portugal.   ISBN 0-941483-33-9   8.95

IN THE BLOOD by Lauren Wright Douglas. 252 pp. Lesbian
science fiction adventure fantasy   ISBN 0-941483-22-3   8.95

THE BEE'S KISS by Shirley Verel. 216 pp. Delicate, delicious
romance.   ISBN 0-941483-36-3   8.95

RAGING MOTHER MOUNTAIN by Pat Emmerson. 264 pp.
Furosa Firechild's adventures in Wonderland.   ISBN 0-941483-35-5   8.95

IN EVERY PORT by Karin Kallmaker. 228 pp. Jessica's sexy,
adventuresome travels.   ISBN 0-941483-37-7   8.95

OF LOVE AND GLORY by Evelyn Kennedy. 192 pp. Exciting
WWII romance.   ISBN 0-941483-32-0   8.95

CLICKING STONES by Nancy Tyler Glenn. 288 pp. Love
transcending time.   ISBN 0-941483-31-2   9.95

SURVIVING SISTERS by Gail Pass. 252 pp. Powerful love
story.   ISBN 0-941483-16-9   8.95

SOUTH OF THE LINE by Catherine Ennis. 216 pp. Civil War
adventure.   ISBN 0-941483-29-0   8.95

WOMAN PLUS WOMAN by Dolores Klaich. 300 pp. Supurb
Lesbian overview.   ISBN 0-941483-28-2   9.95

SLOW DANCING AT MISS POLLY'S by Sheila Ortiz Taylor.
96 pp. Lesbian Poetry   ISBN 0-941483-30-4   7.95

DOUBLE DAUGHTER by Vicki P. McConnell. 216 pp. A Nyla
Wade Mystery, third in the series.   ISBN 0-941483-26-6   8.95

HEAVY GILT by Delores Klaich. 192 pp. Lesbian detective/
disappearing homophobes/upper class gay society.
                                                ISBN 0-941483-25-8   8.95

THE FINER GRAIN by Denise Ohio. 216 pp. Brilliant young
college lesbian novel.   ISBN 0-941483-11-8   8.95

THE AMAZON TRAIL by Lee Lynch. 216 pp. Life, travel & lore
of famous lesbian author.   ISBN 0-941483-27-4   8.95

HIGH CONTRAST by Jessie Lattimore. 264 pp. Women of the
Crystal Palace.   ISBN 0-941483-17-7   8.95

OCTOBER OBSESSION by Meredith More. Josie's rich, secret
Lesbian life.   ISBN 0-941483-18-5   8.95

LESBIAN CROSSROADS by Ruth Baetz. 276 pp. Contemporary
Lesbian lives.   ISBN 0-941483-21-5   9.95

BEFORE STONEWALL: THE MAKING OF A GAY AND
LESBIAN COMMUNITY by Andrea Weiss & Greta Schiller.
96 pp., 25 illus.   ISBN 0-941483-20-7   7.95

WE WALK THE BACK OF THE TIGER by Patricia A. Murphy.
192 pp. Romantic Lesbian novel/beginning women's movement.
                                                ISBN 0-941483-13-4   8.95

SUNDAY'S CHILD by Joyce Bright. 216 pp. Lesbian athletics, at
last the novel about sports.   ISBN 0-941483-12-6   8.95

OSTEN'S BAY by Zenobia N. Vole. 204 pp. Sizzling adventure
romance set on Bonaire.   ISBN 0-941483-15-0   8.95

LESSONS IN MURDER by Claire McNab. 216 pp. 1st Det. Inspec.
Carol Ashton mystery — erotic tension!.   ISBN 0-941483-14-2   8.95

YELLOWTHROAT by Penny Hayes. 240 pp. Margarita, bandit,
kidnaps Julia.   ISBN 0-941483-10-X   8.95

SAPPHISTRY: THE BOOK OF LESBIAN SEXUALITY by
Pat Califia. 3d edition, revised. 208 pp.   ISBN 0-941483-24-X   8.95

CHERISHED LOVE by Evelyn Kennedy. 192 pp. Erotic
Lesbian love story.   ISBN 0-941483-08-8   8.95

LAST SEPTEMBER by Helen R. Hull. 208 pp. Six stories & a
glorious novella.   ISBN 0-941483-09-6   8.95

THE SECRET IN THE BIRD by Camarin Grae. 312 pp. Striking,
psychological suspense novel.   ISBN 0-941483-05-3   8.95

TO THE LIGHTNING by Catherine Ennis. 208 pp. Romantic
Lesbian 'Robinson Crusoe' adventure.   ISBN 0-941483-06-1   8.95

THE OTHER SIDE OF VENUS by Shirley Verel. 224 pp.
Luminous, romantic love story.   ISBN 0-941483-07-X   8.95

DREAMS AND SWORDS by Katherine V. Forrest. 192 pp.
Romantic, erotic, imaginative stories.   ISBN 0-941483-03-7   8.95

MEMORY BOARD by Jane Rule. 336 pp. Memorable novel
about an aging Lesbian couple.   ISBN 0-941483-02-9   9.95

THE ALWAYS ANONYMOUS BEAST by Lauren Wright
Douglas. 224 pp. A Caitlin Reece mystery. First in a series.
                                           ISBN 0-941483-04-5   8.95

SEARCHING FOR SPRING by Patricia A. Murphy. 224 pp.
Novel about the recovery of love.   ISBN 0-941483-00-2   8.95

DUSTY'S QUEEN OF HEARTS DINER by Lee Lynch. 240 pp.
Romantic blue-collar novel.   ISBN 0-941483-01-0   8.95

PARENTS MATTER by Ann Muller. 240 pp. Parents'
relationships with Lesbian daughters and gay sons.
                                           ISBN 0-930044-91-6   9.95

THE PEARLS by Shelley Smith. 176 pp. Passion and fun in
the Caribbean sun.   ISBN 0-930044-93-2   7.95

MAGDALENA by Sarah Aldridge. 352 pp. Epic Lesbian novel
set on three continents.   ISBN 0-930044-99-1   8.95

THE BLACK AND WHITE OF IT by Ann Allen Shockley.
144 pp. Short stories.   ISBN 0-930044-96-7   7.95

SAY JESUS AND COME TO ME by Ann Allen Shockley. 288
pp. Contemporary romance.   ISBN 0-930044-98-3   8.95

LOVING HER by Ann Allen Shockley. 192 pp. Romantic love
story.   ISBN 0-930044-97-5   7.95

MURDER AT THE NIGHTWOOD BAR by Katherine V. Forrest. 240 pp. A Kate Delafield mystery. Second in a series.
ISBN 0-930044-92-4 8.95

ZOE'S BOOK by Gail Pass. 224 pp. Passionate, obsessive love story.
ISBN 0-930044-95-9 7.95

WINGED DANCER by Camarin Grae. 228 pp. Erotic Lesbian adventure story.
ISBN 0-930044-88-6 8.95

PAZ by Camarin Grae. 336 pp. Romantic Lesbian adventurer with the power to change the world.
ISBN 0-930044-89-4 8.95

SOUL SNATCHER by Camarin Grae. 224 pp. A puzzle, an adventure, a mystery — Lesbian romance.
ISBN 0-930044-90-8 8.95

THE LOVE OF GOOD WOMEN by Isabel Miller. 224 pp. Long-awaited new novel by the author of the beloved *Patience and Sarah*.
ISBN 0-930044-81-9 8.95

THE HOUSE AT PELHAM FALLS by Brenda Weathers. 240 pp. Suspenseful Lesbian ghost story.
ISBN 0-930044-79-7 7.95

HOME IN YOUR HANDS by Lee Lynch. 240 pp. More stories from the author of *Old Dyke Tales*.
ISBN 0-930044-80-0 7.95

EACH HAND A MAP by Anita Skeen. 112 pp. Real-life poems that touch us all.
ISBN 0-930044-82-7 6.95

SURPLUS by Sylvia Stevenson. 342 pp. A classic early Lesbian novel.
ISBN 0-930044-78-9 7.95

PEMBROKE PARK by Michelle Martin. 256 pp. Derring-do and daring romance in Regency England.
ISBN 0-930044-77-0 7.95

THE LONG TRAIL by Penny Hayes. 248 pp. Vivid adventures of two women in love in the old west.
ISBN 0-930044-76-2 8.95

HORIZON OF THE HEART by Shelley Smith. 192 pp. Hot romance in summertime New England.
ISBN 0-930044-75-4 7.95

AN EMERGENCE OF GREEN by Katherine V. Forrest. 288 pp. Powerful novel of sexual discovery.
ISBN 0-930044-69-X 9.95

THE LESBIAN PERIODICALS INDEX edited by Claire Potter. 432 pp. Author & subject index.
ISBN 0-930044-74-6 29.95

DESERT OF THE HEART by Jane Rule. 224 pp. A classic; basis for the movie *Desert Hearts*.
ISBN 0-930044-73-8 8.95

SPRING FORWARD/FALL BACK by Sheila Ortiz Taylor. 288 pp. Literary novel of timeless love.
ISBN 0-930044-70-3 7.95

FOR KEEPS by Elisabeth Nonas. 144 pp. Contemporary novel about losing and finding love.
ISBN 0-930044-71-1 7.95

TORCHLIGHT TO VALHALLA by Gale Wilhelm. 128 pp. Classic novel by a great Lesbian writer.
ISBN 0-930044-68-1 7.95

LESBIAN NUNS: BREAKING SILENCE edited by Rosemary
Curb and Nancy Manahan. 432 pp. Unprecedented autobiographies
of religious life.   ISBN 0-930044-62-2   9.95

THE SWASHBUCKLER by Lee Lynch. 288 pp. Colorful novel
set in Greenwich Village in the sixties.   ISBN 0-930044-66-5   8.95

MISFORTUNE'S FRIEND by Sarah Aldridge. 320 pp. Histori-
cal Lesbian novel set on two continents.   ISBN 0-930044-67-3   7.95

A STUDIO OF ONE'S OWN by Ann Stokes. Edited by
Dolores Klaich. 128 pp. Autobiography.   ISBN 0-930044-64-9   7.95

SEX VARIANT WOMEN IN LITERATURE by Jeannette
Howard Foster. 448 pp. Literary history.   ISBN 0-930044-65-7   8.95

A HOT-EYED MODERATE by Jane Rule. 252 pp. Hard-hitting
essays on gay life; writing; art.   ISBN 0-930044-57-6   7.95

INLAND PASSAGE AND OTHER STORIES by Jane Rule.
288 pp. Wide-ranging new collection.   ISBN 0-930044-56-8   7.95

WE TOO ARE DRIFTING by Gale Wilhelm. 128 pp. Timeless
Lesbian novel, a masterpiece.   ISBN 0-930044-61-4   6.95

AMATEUR CITY by Katherine V. Forrest. 224 pp. A Kate
Delafield mystery. First in a series.   ISBN 0-930044-55-X   8.95

THE SOPHIE HOROWITZ STORY by Sarah Schulman. 176
pp. Engaging novel of madcap intrigue.   ISBN 0-930044-54-1   7.95

THE BURNTON WIDOWS by Vickie P. McConnell. 272 pp. A
Nyla Wade mystery, second in the series.   ISBN 0-930044-52-5   7.95

OLD DYKE TALES by Lee Lynch. 224 pp. Extraordinary
stories of our diverse Lesbian lives.   ISBN 0-930044-51-7   8.95

DAUGHTERS OF A CORAL DAWN by Katherine V. Forrest.
240 pp. Novel set in a Lesbian new world.   ISBN 0-930044-50-9   8.95

AGAINST THE SEASON by Jane Rule. 224 pp. Luminous,
complex novel of interrelationships.   ISBN 0-930044-48-7   8.95

LOVERS IN THE PRESENT AFTERNOON by Kathleen
Fleming. 288 pp. A novel about recovery and growth.
                                                ISBN 0-930044-46-0   8.95

TOOTHPICK HOUSE by Lee Lynch. 264 pp. Love between
two Lesbians of different classes.   ISBN 0-930044-45-2   7.95

MADAME AURORA by Sarah Aldridge. 256 pp. Historical
novel featuring a charismatic "seer."   ISBN 0-930044-44-4   7.95

CURIOUS WINE by Katherine V. Forrest. 176 pp. Passionate
Lesbian love story, a best-seller.   ISBN 0-930044-43-6   8.95

BLACK LESBIAN IN WHITE AMERICA by Anita Cornwell.
141 pp. Stories, essays, autobiography.   ISBN 0-930044-41-X   7.95

CONTRACT WITH THE WORLD by Jane Rule. 340 pp.
Powerful, panoramic novel of gay life.   ISBN 0-930044-28-2   9.95